# Tales of the Whispering Forest

**Fairy tales, Folk tales, Legends & Mythology, Volume 1**

Patrick William Lee

Published by Starlit Tales Publishing, 2024.

TALES OF THE WHISPERING FOREST

**First edition. August 2, 2024.**



ISBN: 979-8227234520

Written by Patrick William Lee.

# Table of Contents

To the guardians of dreams and the seekers of magic.

For those who wander through the whispers of ancient forests, where the trees tell stories and the wind carries secrets.

May you always find the courage to face your fears, the wisdom to uncover hidden truths, and the unity to protect the magic that binds us all.

This tale is for you.

# Chapter 1: The Enchanted Grove

The Whispering Forest was a place of legend, a mystical realm hidden deep within the heart of the countryside. Its ancient trees, towering and thick with age, seemed to breathe with a life all their own, their branches whispering secrets to anyone willing to listen. This forest had stood for millennia, a silent witness to the passage of time, guarding its mysteries and stories within its shadowy depths. It was said that only those pure of heart could truly understand the forest's whispers, and among those chosen few were two young children: Elara and Finn.

Elara was a brave young girl with fiery red hair and a spirit to match. She was known in her village for her courage and kindness, often leading the other children on adventures through the fields and woods near their homes. Her best friend, Finn, was a curious boy with an insatiable thirst for knowledge. His sandy blonde hair and bright blue eyes gave him an innocent appearance, but his mind was always racing with questions and ideas. Together, they made a formidable pair, each balancing the other's strengths and weaknesses.

The story of their journey began on a warm summer day, when the sun hung high in the sky, casting dappled light through the leaves of the Whispering Forest. The air was filled with the sounds of nature: the chirping of birds, the rustle of leaves, and the distant murmur of a stream. Elara and Finn had ventured deeper into the forest than ever before, drawn by an inexplicable sense of adventure.

Their animal companions, a clever fox named Vixen and a loyal dog named Max, trotted alongside them. Vixen, with her sleek orange fur and sharp, intelligent eyes, was always alert, sensing danger before it could strike. Max, a sturdy brown and white dog, was fearless and fiercely protective of his human friends. The four of them had faced many small adventures together, but nothing could have prepared them for what lay ahead.

As they walked, Elara and Finn marveled at the forest's beauty. The trees here were unlike any they had seen before, their bark etched with strange, swirling patterns that seemed to move when glanced at out of the corner of the eye. Moss and ivy climbed their trunks, creating a tapestry of green that softened the forest floor. Sunlight filtered through the canopy, casting a golden glow that gave the forest an otherworldly feel.

"Do you hear that, Elara?" Finn asked, stopping suddenly and cocking his head to one side.

Elara paused and listened. At first, she heard nothing unusual, just the typical sounds of the forest. But then, faint and distant, she caught a soft, melodic whisper. It was as if the trees themselves were speaking, their voices merging into a harmonious chorus.

"I do," she replied, her eyes widening with wonder. "It's like the forest is trying to tell us something."

Vixen's ears perked up, and Max growled softly, sensing that something significant was about to happen. The animals, too, seemed to feel the forest's energy shifting around them.

Curiosity piqued, the children continued their journey, following the whispers that grew louder with each step. The path before them was barely visible, overgrown with ferns and wildflowers, but they pressed on, driven by an unseen force. The deeper they went, the more magical the forest became. Flowers with petals that glowed in the shade, mushrooms that sparkled with dew, and trees that seemed to bend toward them, as if guiding their way.

After what felt like hours, they arrived at a small clearing. In the center stood an ancient grove, unlike anything they had ever seen. The trees here were older and larger, their trunks as wide as cottages, and their branches forming a dense canopy overhead. The air was thick with the scent of pine and earth, and a gentle breeze rustled the leaves, creating a soothing symphony.

Elara stepped forward, her eyes fixed on the largest tree in the grove. Its bark was silver, and its leaves shimmered with an ethereal light. As she approached, she felt a strange sensation, like the tree was calling to her, beckoning her closer.

"Finn, look at this," she whispered, her voice barely audible above the rustling leaves.

Finn joined her, his eyes wide with awe. "It's beautiful," he breathed. "I've never seen anything like it."

Vixen and Max sat quietly at their feet, their eyes fixed on the tree as if they, too, felt its power. There was something magical about this grove, something that felt ancient and wise.

As they stood there, mesmerized by the tree's beauty, a voice broke the silence. It was soft and melodious, like the whispers of the forest itself.

"Welcome, children," it said. "You have found the heart of the Whispering Forest."

Elara and Finn looked around, trying to find the source of the voice, but saw no one. The voice seemed to come from everywhere and nowhere at once.

"Who are you?" Elara asked, her voice trembling with a mixture of fear and excitement.

"I am the spirit of the forest," the voice replied. "I have watched over this land for centuries, guarding its secrets and protecting its inhabitants. You have been chosen to hear my voice because of your pure hearts and brave spirits."

Finn stepped forward, his curiosity overcoming his fear. "Why have you called us here?" he asked. "What do you want us to do?"

The forest spirit's voice grew softer, almost sad. "The forest is in danger," it said. "A darkness is spreading, threatening to consume everything in its path. I need your help to stop it."

Elara and Finn exchanged worried glances. They had heard stories of the forest's magic, but they had never imagined it would be up to them to protect it.

"What can we do?" Elara asked, her voice determined. "We're just children."

"You are more powerful than you know," the spirit replied. "The magic of the forest flows through you, and together, you can save it. But you must be brave and trust in yourselves."

Finn nodded, his resolve strengthening. "We will do whatever it takes," he said. "We won't let the darkness win."

The spirit's voice grew stronger, filled with hope. "Thank you, children," it said. "Your journey will not be easy, but I believe in you. Remember, the forest will always be with you, guiding and protecting you."

With that, the voice faded, leaving Elara and Finn standing in the grove, their hearts pounding with a mixture of fear and excitement. They had been chosen to save the Whispering Forest, and they were ready to face whatever challenges lay ahead.

As they left the grove, they felt a renewed sense of purpose. The whispers of the forest seemed to follow them, encouraging and guiding them. They knew their journey would be difficult, but they were determined to protect the magical land they loved.

With Vixen and Max by their side, they set off into the depths of the Whispering Forest, ready to face the darkness and uncover the secrets that lay hidden within its ancient trees. Their adventure had only just begun, and they were prepared to face whatever trials awaited them, knowing that the spirit of the forest was always with them, whispering its wisdom and strength.

# Chapter 2: The Legend of the Whispering Trees

The Whispering Forest had always been a place of mystery and magic, its secrets guarded by the ancient trees that towered over the land. As Elara and Finn ventured deeper into the forest, the whispers grew louder, filling their minds with a strange sense of familiarity and wonder. They knew that the forest held many secrets, and they were determined to uncover them.

It was a cool autumn morning when they set out on their quest. The sun hung low in the sky, casting long shadows through the trees. Leaves of gold, red, and orange carpeted the forest floor, crunching underfoot as they walked. The air was crisp and filled with the earthy scent of fallen leaves and damp soil.

Elara and Finn had decided to visit the oldest part of the forest, a place known as the Eldertree Glade. It was said that the trees there were the first to grow in the forest, and that they held the wisdom of the ages within their gnarled branches and deep roots. Their journey was guided by the whispers of the forest, which seemed to grow more insistent with each passing day.

As they walked, Vixen and Max trotted beside them, their eyes alert and ears perked. The forest was alive with the sounds of nature: the rustling of leaves, the chirping of birds, and the distant call of a deer. But beneath these sounds, Elara and Finn could hear the whispers, faint and melodic, like a song carried on the wind.

"Do you ever wonder what the whispers are saying?" Finn asked, breaking the silence.

Elara nodded. "I think they're trying to tell us something important," she replied. "Something about the forest and its history. We just have to listen carefully."

As they continued their journey, the trees grew taller and more ancient, their bark covered in thick moss and twisted vines. The whispers grew louder, almost as if the trees themselves were speaking to them. It was then that they saw it: the entrance to the Eldertree Glade.

The glade was a circular clearing surrounded by towering trees, their branches interwoven to form a natural canopy. Sunlight filtered through the leaves, casting dappled shadows on the ground. In the center of the glade stood the Eldertree, a massive oak with a trunk as wide as a house and branches that reached high into the sky. Its bark was silver-gray and etched with intricate patterns that seemed to shift and change as the light played across them.

Elara and Finn approached the Eldertree with a sense of reverence. They could feel the ancient power emanating from the tree, a deep, pulsing energy that resonated with their own hearts. As they stood before the tree, the whispers grew louder, filling their minds with a symphony of voices.

"Welcome, children," a voice said, breaking the silence. It was soft and melodic, like the rustling of leaves in the wind. "You have come seeking the wisdom of the Whispering Trees."

Elara and Finn looked around, trying to find the source of the voice. To their surprise, it seemed to come from the Eldertree itself.

"Are you... the spirit of the forest?" Finn asked, his voice filled with awe.

"I am one of the guardian spirits of this forest," the voice replied. "I have watched over these trees for centuries, guiding and protecting them. You have been chosen to hear my voice because of your pure hearts and brave spirits."

Elara stepped forward, her eyes wide with wonder. "We want to learn about the forest and its history," she said. "We want to understand the whispers and help protect this place."

The Eldertree's branches swayed gently, as if nodding in agreement. "There is much to learn, and many stories to tell," the voice said. "But first, you must meet someone who can help you understand the forest's past."

As the words faded, a figure emerged from the shadows at the edge of the glade. It was an old man, dressed in tattered robes and leaning on a wooden staff. His hair was long and silver, and his eyes sparkled with a mischievous light. He looked like he had stepped out of a fairy tale, a living embodiment of the forest's ancient magic.

"Greetings, young ones," the old man said, his voice warm and friendly. "I am known as Aelric, the storyteller. I have lived in this forest for many years, listening to its whispers and learning its secrets. I have many tales to share, if you are willing to listen."

Elara and Finn nodded eagerly, their curiosity piqued. They sat down on the soft grass, their eyes fixed on Aelric as he began his tale.

"Long ago," Aelric began, "this forest was a place of great magic and wonder. The trees were young and full of life, and the land was teeming with creatures of all kinds. The forest was protected by powerful guardian spirits, who watched over the trees and kept the balance of nature in harmony."

He paused, his eyes distant as he recalled the ancient memories. "But there was one tree, the Eldertree, that was different from all the others. It was the first tree to grow in the forest, and it held within its roots the wisdom of the ages. The Eldertree was a bridge between the mortal world and the spirit realm, and it whispered its wisdom to those who could hear."

Elara and Finn listened intently, their minds filled with images of the ancient forest. "What happened to the guardian spirits?" Elara asked. "Are they still here?"

Aelric nodded. "Yes, the guardian spirits are still here, watching over the forest. But their power has waned over the centuries, and the balance of nature has been threatened by dark forces. That is why the forest called to you, to help restore the balance and protect this magical place."

Finn leaned forward, his eyes wide with excitement. "What kind of dark forces?" he asked. "And how can we help?"

Aelric's expression grew serious. "There are many dangers that threaten the forest," he said. "Some come from the outside world, from those who seek to exploit the land for their own gain. Others come from within, from creatures and spirits that have been corrupted by dark magic. To protect the forest, you must learn to listen to the whispers and understand the wisdom of the trees."

He paused, his eyes scanning the glade. "There is a legend," he continued, "that speaks of a great hero who will come to the forest in its time of need. This hero will have the ability to hear the whispers of the trees and the strength to stand against the darkness. I believe that you, Elara and Finn, are the heroes foretold in the legend."

Elara and Finn exchanged glances, their hearts pounding with a mixture of fear and excitement. They had always dreamed of going on a grand adventure, but they had never imagined it would be like this.

"What do we need to do?" Elara asked, her voice filled with determination.

"You must learn to understand the whispers of the trees," Aelric said. "They will guide you on your journey and help you uncover the secrets of the forest. But be warned, the path ahead will not be easy. You will face many challenges and dangers, but if you stay true to your hearts and trust in each other, you will succeed."

He reached into his robes and pulled out a small, intricately carved wooden amulet. "Take this," he said, handing it to Elara. "It is a talisman of protection, crafted from the wood of the Eldertree. It will help you hear the whispers and protect you from harm."

Elara took the amulet, feeling its smooth surface and the warmth of its magic. She slipped it over her head, feeling a sense of comfort and strength.

"Thank you, Aelric," she said, her voice filled with gratitude. "We will do our best to protect the forest and restore the balance."

Aelric smiled, his eyes twinkling with pride. "I know you will," he said. "Now, go forth and listen to the whispers. The forest will guide you on your journey."

With that, Elara and Finn stood up, their hearts filled with determination. They had a purpose, a mission to protect the Whispering Forest and uncover its secrets. As they left the Eldertree Glade, the whispers grew louder, filling their minds with a symphony of voices.

They walked in silence for a while, each lost in their own thoughts. The forest around them seemed to come alive, the trees swaying gently as if acknowledging their presence.

"What do you think the whispers are trying to tell us?" Finn asked, breaking the silence.

"I don't know," Elara replied. "But I feel like they're guiding us somewhere. We just have to keep listening and trust in the forest."

As they continued their journey, they felt a sense of unity with the forest, as if they were part of something much larger than themselves. The whispers seemed to speak directly to their hearts, filling them with wisdom and strength.

Days turned into weeks as they traveled through the Whispering Forest, guided by the whispers and protected by the talisman. They encountered many challenges along the way, from treacherous terrain to dangerous creatures. But with each trial, they grew stronger and more confident in their abilities.

One evening, as they were setting up camp by a small stream, they heard a rustling in the bushes. Vixen and Max immediately sprang to attention, their ears perked and eyes alert.

"Who's there?" Elara called out, her hand reaching for the amulet around her neck.

To their surprise, a young woman stepped out from the shadows. She was dressed in simple clothing, her dark hair flowing freely around her shoulders. Her eyes were a deep, mossy green, and she had an air of mystery about her.

"Peace, friends," she said, raising her hands in a gesture of goodwill. "I mean you no harm. My name is Liora, and I have been watching your journey."

Elara and Finn exchanged glances, their curiosity piqued. "Why have you been watching us?" Finn asked.

Liora smiled, her eyes sparkling with warmth. "I am one of the forest's guardians," she said. "I have been sent to guide you and help you on your quest."

Elara's eyes widened in surprise. "You're a guardian spirit?" she asked.

Liora nodded. "Yes, though I am not as powerful as the ancient spirits. I am a protector of the forest, and I have been watching over you since you entered the Eldertree Glade."

Finn stepped forward, his curiosity getting the better of him. "Can you tell us more about the guardian spirits and the history of the forest?" he asked.

Liora's expression grew serious. "There is much to tell, and not all of it is pleasant," she said. "But you must understand the past to protect the future."

She sat down on a fallen log, gesturing for Elara and Finn to join her. Vixen and Max lay down at their feet, their eyes fixed on Liora as she began her tale.

"Long ago, before the forest was known as the Whispering Forest, it was a place of great power and beauty," Liora began. "The trees were young and full of life, and the land was teeming with creatures of all kinds. The forest was protected by powerful guardian spirits, who watched over the trees and kept the balance of nature in harmony."

She paused, her eyes distant as she recalled the ancient memories. "The guardian spirits were beings of great wisdom and strength, each with their own unique abilities. They could communicate with the trees, the animals, and the elements, ensuring that the forest thrived and flourished."

Liora's expression grew somber. "But not all was peaceful in the forest. There were dark forces that sought to corrupt and destroy the harmony of nature. These forces came from within and without, from creatures and spirits that had been twisted by dark magic and from those who sought to exploit the land for their own gain."

Elara and Finn listened intently, their minds filled with images of the ancient forest and the battles that had been fought to protect it.

"The guardian spirits fought bravely to defend the forest," Liora continued. "But the darkness was strong, and many spirits were lost in the struggle. The balance of nature was threatened, and the forest began to wither and die."

Her voice grew softer, filled with sadness. "It was during this time of great turmoil that the Eldertree, the first tree to grow in the forest, revealed its true power. The Eldertree was a bridge between the mortal world and the spirit realm, and it held within its roots the wisdom of the ages. It whispered its wisdom to those who could hear, guiding and protecting them."

Liora's eyes met Elara's, her gaze intense. "The legend speaks of a great hero who will come to the forest in its time of need. This hero will have the ability to hear the whispers of the trees and the strength to stand against the darkness. I believe that you, Elara and Finn, are the heroes foretold in the legend."

Elara and Finn exchanged glances, their hearts pounding with a mixture of fear and excitement. They had always dreamed of going on a grand adventure, but they had never imagined it would be like this.

"What do we need to do?" Elara asked, her voice filled with determination.

"You must learn to understand the whispers of the trees," Liora said. "They will guide you on your journey and help you uncover the secrets of the forest. But be warned, the path ahead will not be easy. You will face many challenges and dangers, but if you stay true to your hearts and trust in each other, you will succeed."

She reached into her bag and pulled out a small, intricately carved wooden amulet. "Take this," she said, handing it to Finn. "It is a talisman of protection, crafted from the wood of the Eldertree. It will help you hear the whispers and protect you from harm."

Finn took the amulet, feeling its smooth surface and the warmth of its magic. He slipped it over his head, feeling a sense of comfort and strength.

"Thank you, Liora," he said, his voice filled with gratitude. "We will do our best to protect the forest and restore the balance."

Liora smiled, her eyes twinkling with pride. "I know you will," she said. "Now, go forth and listen to the whispers. The forest will guide you on your journey."

With that, Elara and Finn stood up, their hearts filled with determination. They had a purpose, a mission to protect the Whispering Forest and uncover its secrets. As they left the glade, the whispers grew louder, filling their minds with a symphony of voices.

Their journey was far from over, but they felt a renewed sense of hope and purpose. They knew that the forest held many challenges and dangers, but they were ready to face them together. With Vixen and Max by their side, and the guidance of the guardian spirits, they set off into the depths of the Whispering Forest, ready to uncover its secrets and protect its ancient magic.

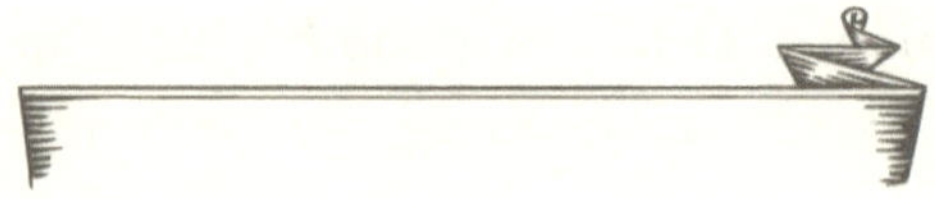

# Chapter 3: The Quest for the Silver Leaf

The Whispering Forest had always been a place of wonder and mystery, but now it was more than that—it was a place of destiny. Elara and Finn had been chosen by the ancient guardian spirits to embark on a quest to find the legendary Silver Leaf. According to the legend, the Silver Leaf held the power to communicate directly with the forest, a gift that could help them protect the land from the encroaching darkness. With Vixen the fox and Max the loyal dog by their side, they set off on their journey with hearts full of determination and minds full of questions.

The whispers of the forest seemed to guide their every step, growing louder and more insistent as they made their way through the dense foliage. The trees towered above them, their branches interwoven to form a natural canopy that filtered the sunlight into a soft, golden glow. The air was thick with the scent of pine and earth, and the sounds of nature created a soothing symphony that accompanied their journey.

As they walked, Elara and Finn discussed the legend of the Silver Leaf and the challenges they might face. They knew that the quest would not be easy, but they were ready to face whatever trials awaited them.

"The Silver Leaf is said to be hidden deep within the heart of the forest," Finn said, his voice filled with excitement. "But no one knows exactly where it is or what challenges we might face along the way."

Elara nodded, her eyes scanning the forest around them. "We just have to keep listening to the whispers and trust in the forest," she replied. "The guardian spirits will guide us."

Their journey took them through some of the most beautiful and enchanting parts of the Whispering Forest. They passed through groves of ancient trees whose bark was etched with intricate patterns, crossed clear streams that sparkled in the sunlight, and navigated dense thickets of ferns and wildflowers. Everywhere they went, they felt the presence of the forest's magic, a constant reminder of the importance of their quest.

After several days of travel, they reached the edge of a wide, shimmering river. The River of Reflection was known for its calm, mirror-like surface that reflected the sky and trees with perfect clarity. According to the whispers, this was the first major challenge on their quest for the Silver Leaf.

Elara and Finn stood on the riverbank, gazing at the water with a mixture of awe and trepidation. The river was wide and deep, and there was no visible way to cross it. The whispers of the forest grew louder, urging them to find a way.

"The River of Reflection is said to test those who seek to cross it," Elara said, her voice thoughtful. "We have to find a way to prove our worthiness."

Finn nodded, his mind racing with ideas. "Maybe there's a hidden bridge or a magical way to cross," he suggested. "We just have to figure out what the river wants from us."

They explored the riverbank, looking for any clues or signs that might help them. Vixen and Max trotted alongside them, their eyes alert and ears perked. The animals seemed to sense the importance of the moment, their usual playful energy replaced with a focused determination.

After some time, Finn noticed something unusual about the reflection in the water. "Elara, look at this," he called, pointing to a spot where the reflection seemed to shimmer and change.

Elara joined him, her eyes widening in surprise. The reflection in the water was not just mirroring the trees and sky—it was showing something else, a hidden path that seemed to lead across the river.

"It's a bridge made of light," Elara whispered, her voice filled with wonder. "But how do we make it real?"

As they pondered the question, the whispers of the forest grew even louder, filling their minds with a single, clear thought: "Look within."

Elara and Finn exchanged glances, understanding dawning in their eyes. The River of Reflection was not just a physical challenge—it was a test of their inner strength and self-awareness. They had to look within themselves to find the answers they sought.

Elara closed her eyes, taking a deep breath and centering her thoughts. She focused on her connection to the forest, the whispers that had guided her, and the strength she felt within her heart. As she did, she felt a warm, tingling sensation in her chest, a glow that seemed to spread throughout her body.

Finn did the same, closing his eyes and reaching deep within himself. He focused on his curiosity, his desire to learn and explore, and the bond he shared with Elara and their animal companions. He, too, felt the warmth and glow, a light that seemed to radiate from his very being.

As they opened their eyes, they saw that the shimmering path in the water had become solid, a bridge of light that spanned the river. The whispers of the forest seemed to cheer them on, their voices filled with encouragement and pride.

"Let's go," Elara said, her voice steady and determined. She took Finn's hand, and together they stepped onto the bridge of light.

The sensation was surreal, as if they were walking on air. The bridge was solid beneath their feet, but it seemed to pulse with a life of its own, glowing with an ethereal light. Vixen and Max followed closely, their steps sure and confident.

As they reached the other side of the river, the bridge of light faded away, leaving them standing on the opposite bank. They had passed the first challenge, proving their worthiness and inner strength.

The forest around them seemed to come alive with a renewed sense of magic and energy. The trees whispered their approval, and the air was filled with the sweet scent of blooming flowers. Elara and Finn felt a surge of confidence, knowing that they were on the right path.

Their journey continued, guided by the whispers and the wisdom of the forest. They faced many challenges along the way, each one testing their courage, intelligence, and bond with the forest. They encountered treacherous terrain, cunning creatures, and ancient puzzles that required all their skills to solve.

One such challenge came in the form of a dark, twisted thicket that seemed impenetrable. The whispers guided them to a hidden entrance, a narrow passage that led into the heart of the thicket. As they ventured deeper, they found themselves in a labyrinth of thorny vines and shadowy paths.

The air was thick with tension, and the whispers grew softer, as if the forest itself was holding its breath. Elara and Finn knew that they had to rely on their instincts and their bond with each other to navigate the maze.

"We have to stay together and trust each other," Elara said, her voice steady. "The forest will guide us if we listen."

Finn nodded, his eyes scanning the shadows for any sign of danger. Vixen and Max stayed close, their senses on high alert. The thicket seemed to close in around them, the vines reaching out like twisted fingers.

As they made their way through the labyrinth, they encountered several dead ends and false paths. Each time, they had to backtrack and find a new way, relying on the whispers and their intuition. The journey was slow and challenging, but they never lost hope.

After what felt like hours, they finally emerged from the thicket into a small clearing. In the center of the clearing stood a stone pedestal, and atop it rested a shimmering leaf made of pure silver. The Silver Leaf.

Elara and Finn approached the pedestal with a sense of awe and reverence. The Silver Leaf glowed with an ethereal light, its surface etched with intricate patterns that seemed to shift and change. They could feel its magic, a deep, resonant energy that filled the air.

"We found it," Finn whispered, his voice filled with wonder. "The Silver Leaf."

Elara reached out, her hand trembling slightly as she touched the leaf. The moment her fingers made contact, a surge of energy flowed through her, connecting her to the forest in a way she had never felt before. She could hear the whispers more clearly, their voices filled with wisdom and guidance.

Finn placed his hand on the leaf as well, and he, too, felt the connection. It was as if the forest was speaking directly to them, sharing its secrets and its strength.

"With this, we can communicate with the forest," Elara said, her voice filled with determination. "We can protect it from the darkness."

Finn nodded, his eyes shining with resolve. "We will do whatever it takes," he said. "Together, we can save the Whispering Forest."

As they took the Silver Leaf, the clearing seemed to come alive with a burst of magic. The trees swayed gently, their leaves rustling in a melodic chorus. The air was filled with the sweet scent of blooming flowers, and the ground beneath their feet seemed to hum with energy.

Elara and Finn knew that their quest was far from over, but they felt a renewed sense of hope and purpose. With the Silver Leaf in their possession, they had the power to communicate with the forest and uncover its secrets. They were ready to face whatever challenges lay ahead, knowing that the guardian spirits and the wisdom of the Whispering Forest were with them.

Their journey back through the thicket was much easier, guided by the whispers and the magic of the Silver Leaf. The twisted vines seemed to part before them, creating a clear path that led them back to the river.

As they reached the River of Reflection once more, they found the bridge of light waiting for them, shimmering and solid. They crossed it with confidence, knowing that they had proven their worthiness.

The other side of the river seemed even more vibrant and alive than before. The trees whispered their approval, and the animals of the forest seemed to greet them with newfound respect. Elara and Finn felt a deep connection to the land, a bond that had been strengthened by their quest.

They continued their journey, guided by the whispers and the wisdom of the Silver Leaf. They encountered many more challenges and dangers, but each one only served to strengthen their resolve and their bond with the forest.

One particularly memorable challenge came in the form of a shadowy figure that appeared one evening as they set up camp. The figure was cloaked in darkness, its eyes glowing with an eerie light.

"Who are you?" Elara demanded, stepping forward with the Silver Leaf in hand.

The figure laughed, a cold, mocking sound that sent shivers down their spines. "I am a servant of the darkness," it said. "And I have come to claim the Silver Leaf for my master."

Finn stepped forward, his eyes blazing with determination. "You will not take it," he said. "We will protect the forest and its magic."

The shadowy figure lunged at them, but Elara and Finn stood their ground. The Silver Leaf glowed with a brilliant light, repelling the darkness and filling the clearing with a radiant energy.

The figure hissed in anger, retreating into the shadows. "This is not over," it snarled. "The darkness will consume you all."

Elara and Finn watched as the figure disappeared, their hearts pounding with a mixture of fear and determination. They knew that the darkness was a formidable enemy, but they were ready to face it head-on.

"We have to stay strong," Elara said, her voice steady. "The forest is counting on us."

Finn nodded, his eyes filled with resolve. "We won't let the darkness win," he said. "We'll protect the Whispering Forest with everything we have."

As they continued their journey, they encountered many more challenges, each one testing their courage, intelligence, and bond with the forest. They faced treacherous terrain, cunning creatures, and ancient puzzles that required all their skills to solve.

One such challenge came in the form of a hidden cave that they discovered deep within the forest. The entrance was concealed by a waterfall, and the whispers guided them to it.

Inside the cave, they found a series of ancient carvings that told the story of the forest and its guardian spirits. The carvings depicted battles with dark forces, the creation of the Silver Leaf, and the legend of the chosen heroes who would save the forest in its time of need.

Elara and Finn studied the carvings carefully, learning more about the history of the Whispering Forest and the challenges that lay ahead. They felt a deep sense of responsibility, knowing that they were part of a long line of protectors who had dedicated their lives to safeguarding the land.

As they left the cave, they felt a renewed sense of purpose and determination. The whispers of the forest guided them, filling their minds with wisdom and strength. They knew that their journey was far from over, but they were ready to face whatever challenges lay ahead.

Their quest for the Silver Leaf had brought them closer to the heart of the Whispering Forest and had strengthened their bond with the land. They had proven their worthiness and had gained the power to communicate with the forest, a gift that would help them protect it from the darkness.

Elara and Finn walked side by side, their hearts filled with hope and resolve. With Vixen and Max by their side, they were ready to face whatever trials awaited them. The whispers of the forest guided them, a constant reminder of the magic and wisdom that surrounded them.

As they continued their journey, they knew that they were not alone. The guardian spirits watched over them, and the wisdom of the Whispering Forest filled their hearts. They were ready to protect the land they loved and to uncover the secrets that lay hidden within its ancient trees.

Their adventure was far from over, but they faced it with courage and determination. The quest for the Silver Leaf had only just begun, and they were ready to embrace the challenges and triumphs that lay ahead. Together, they would protect the Whispering Forest and ensure that its magic and wisdom would endure for generations to come.

# Chapter 4: The Trickster Fox

The Whispering Forest was a realm of boundless wonders and hidden dangers, and as Elara and Finn continued their quest, they quickly realized that not everything was as it seemed. Guided by the whispers and protected by the Silver Leaf, they had already faced numerous challenges. However, nothing could have prepared them for their encounter with the Trickster Fox.

It was a crisp autumn morning when they first met him. The sun was just beginning to rise, casting a golden glow through the trees and illuminating the dew-covered ground. The air was filled with the scent of pine and earth, and the forest was alive with the sounds of birds chirping and leaves rustling in the breeze.

Elara and Finn were following a narrow path that wound through a dense thicket of trees. Vixen, their clever fox companion, trotted ahead, her nose to the ground as she sniffed out their path. Max, the loyal dog, walked beside Elara, his ears perked and eyes alert.

As they rounded a bend in the path, they came across a small clearing. In the center of the clearing stood a fox, larger and more striking than any they had ever seen. His fur was a deep, rich red, and his eyes glowed with a mischievous light. He sat on his haunches, watching them with a sly smile.

"Greetings, travelers," the fox said, his voice smooth and melodic. "I am known as Reynard, the Trickster Fox. I have been watching your journey, and I believe I can be of assistance."

Elara and Finn exchanged glances, their curiosity piqued. They had heard tales of Reynard, a cunning and clever fox who was known for his tricks and deceptions. He was a legendary figure in the forest, both feared and admired for his intelligence and wit.

"We appreciate your offer," Elara said cautiously. "But we have heard that you are not always to be trusted."

Reynard's smile widened, and he let out a low chuckle. "Ah, my reputation precedes me," he said. "But I assure you, my intentions are noble. I have valuable knowledge and skills that can aid you on your quest. All I ask in return is a small favor."

Finn raised an eyebrow, skeptical but intrigued. "What kind of favor?" he asked.

Reynard's eyes twinkled with amusement. "Nothing too difficult," he replied. "There is a rare herb that grows deep within the forest, known as the Moonflower. It blooms only under the light of the full moon and is said to have magical properties. I need this herb for a special potion I am brewing. If you help me find it, I will guide you through the maze of illusions that lies ahead."

Elara and Finn considered the offer. They knew that the maze of illusions was a dangerous and confusing place, and having Reynard's guidance could be invaluable. However, they also knew that the Trickster Fox was not to be trusted lightly.

"We will help you find the Moonflower," Elara said finally. "But we need your word that you will guide us safely through the maze."

Reynard bowed his head, his expression serious. "You have my word," he said. "I will lead you safely through the maze, and in return, you will help me find the Moonflower. Do we have a deal?"

Elara and Finn nodded, and the deal was struck. With that, Reynard led them deeper into the forest, his movements graceful and sure. The path grew narrower and more twisted, the trees closing in around them as they ventured further into the heart of the forest.

As they walked, Reynard regaled them with tales of his adventures and exploits. He spoke of the many tricks he had played on both friend and foe, and the lessons he had learned along the way. Elara and Finn listened with a mixture of fascination and caution, aware that the Trickster Fox was as much a storyteller as he was a trickster.

After several hours of walking, they reached the entrance to the maze of illusions. It was an eerie and foreboding place, with tall hedges that seemed to stretch endlessly in every direction. The air was thick with an otherworldly mist, and the whispers of the forest seemed to grow fainter, replaced by strange and unsettling sounds.

"This is where our journey becomes more challenging," Reynard said, his voice serious. "The maze is a place of deception and confusion. It will test your wits and your resolve. But fear not, for I will guide you through it."

With that, they entered the maze, the tall hedges closing in around them like walls. The path was narrow and winding, and the mist made it difficult to see more than a few feet ahead. Reynard led the way, his movements confident and sure, while Elara and Finn followed closely behind, their eyes and ears alert for any sign of danger.

As they ventured deeper into the maze, they encountered a series of illusions designed to confuse and deceive them. The first illusion was a beautiful meadow filled with flowers and sunlight. It seemed like a paradise, but Reynard warned them that it was a trap.

"Do not be fooled by appearances," he said. "This meadow is an illusion meant to lure you into a false sense of security. We must continue forward and stay focused on our goal."

They pressed on, leaving the meadow behind. The path grew darker and more twisted, the mist thickening around them. The second illusion they encountered was a shadowy figure that appeared to block their path. It was a menacing creature with glowing red eyes and sharp claws, and it seemed intent on stopping them.

"Stand your ground and do not be afraid," Reynard said calmly. "This creature is an illusion, a manifestation of your fears. It cannot harm you if you do not allow it to."

Elara and Finn took a deep breath and stood their ground, their hearts pounding with fear. The shadowy figure advanced, its claws raised, but as they held their ground, it began to fade, dissolving into the mist.

"Well done," Reynard said, nodding in approval. "You have faced your fears and seen through the illusion. We must continue forward."

They moved deeper into the maze, the path growing more convoluted and confusing. The mist swirled around them, creating strange and disorienting patterns. The third illusion they encountered was a mirror image of themselves, standing in their path and mimicking their every move.

"This is a test of your self-awareness," Reynard said. "You must recognize that what you see is not real, but a reflection of your own doubts and uncertainties. Trust in yourselves and move forward."

Elara and Finn stared at their mirror images, feeling a strange sense of unease. The reflections seemed so real, so lifelike, but they knew that they were just illusions. They took a step forward, and the reflections did the same. They took another step, and the reflections followed.

"Do not be afraid to confront your own reflection," Reynard said. "Only by facing your inner self can you move past this illusion."

Elara and Finn took a deep breath and stepped forward boldly. As they did, the mirror images began to waver and dissolve, fading into the mist. They had passed another test, and the path ahead became clearer.

"Excellent," Reynard said, his eyes twinkling with approval. "You are learning to see through the illusions and trust in yourselves. We are almost through the maze."

They continued forward, the mist growing thinner as they neared the center of the maze. The path became less convoluted, and the whispers of the forest began to return, guiding them forward.

As they reached the heart of the maze, they found themselves in a small clearing. In the center of the clearing stood a tall, ancient tree with silver leaves that shimmered in the sunlight. The tree seemed to glow with an ethereal light, and the air around it was filled with a sense of peace and magic.

"This is the Moonflower Tree," Reynard said, his voice filled with reverence. "The Moonflower blooms only under the light of the full moon, and its petals hold powerful magic. We must wait for nightfall to harvest the herb."

Elara and Finn nodded, their eyes fixed on the tree. They could feel its magic, a deep, resonant energy that filled the air. They knew that they had reached an important milestone in their journey, but they also knew that their quest was far from over.

As they waited for nightfall, Reynard spoke to them about the lessons they had learned in the maze. "The maze of illusions is a test of trust and deception," he said. "It teaches you to see through appearances and recognize the truth. You have done well, but remember that trust is a double-edged sword. You must learn to discern who is worthy of your trust and who is not."

Elara and Finn listened intently, taking his words to heart. They had faced many challenges and learned valuable lessons, but they knew that the Trickster Fox was not to be trusted lightly. They would need to stay vigilant and keep their wits about them as they continued their journey.

As night fell, the full moon rose high in the sky, casting a silver light over the clearing. The Moonflower Tree began to glow, its silver leaves shimmering in the moonlight. Slowly, delicate white flowers began to bloom, their petals glowing with an otherworldly light.

Reynard approached the tree with a sense of reverence, carefully plucking the flowers and placing them in a small pouch. "These will be perfect for my potion," he said, his eyes filled with satisfaction. "You have upheld your end of the bargain, and now I will uphold mine. I will guide you safely through the rest of the maze and lead you to the next part of

your journey."

Elara and Finn watched as Reynard carefully harvested the Moonflowers, their hearts filled with a mixture of relief and caution. They had completed their task and earned his guidance, but they knew that the Trickster Fox was not to be trusted completely.

With the Moonflowers safely stored, Reynard led them back through the maze, guiding them with confidence and skill. The illusions seemed to part before them, the path becoming clearer with each step. Elara and Finn felt a sense of accomplishment, knowing that they had passed the tests and learned valuable lessons along the way.

As they emerged from the maze, the whispers of the forest grew louder, welcoming them back with a sense of approval. They had faced their fears, seen through the illusions, and proven their worthiness. The forest recognized their determination and rewarded them with its guidance and protection.

Reynard turned to them with a smile, his eyes twinkling with a mixture of amusement and respect. "You have done well, young heroes," he said. "You have learned valuable lessons about trust and deception, and you have proven yourselves worthy of the forest's magic. Remember these lessons as you continue your journey, for they will serve you well."

Elara and Finn thanked Reynard for his guidance, their hearts filled with gratitude and caution. They had learned to see through appearances and recognize the truth, but they knew that their journey was far from over. They would need to stay vigilant and trust in themselves as they faced the challenges ahead.

With Vixen and Max by their side, they continued their journey through the Whispering Forest, guided by the whispers and the wisdom of the Silver Leaf. They knew that they were not alone, and that the guardian spirits and the magic of the forest were with them. They were ready to face whatever trials awaited them, knowing that they had the strength and the determination to succeed.

Their adventure was far from over, but they faced it with courage and resolve. The encounter with the Trickster Fox had taught them valuable lessons about trust and deception, and they were stronger for it. Together, they would protect the Whispering Forest and ensure that its magic and wisdom would endure for generations to come.

# Chapter 5: The Hidden Village

The Whispering Forest held countless secrets within its ancient depths, secrets that Elara and Finn were only beginning to uncover. Having successfully navigated the maze of illusions with the help of the Trickster Fox, they felt more determined than ever to protect the forest and its magic. As they ventured deeper into the heart of the forest, they stumbled upon one of its greatest secrets—a hidden village inhabited by forest spirits and magical creatures.

It was a clear, crisp morning when they set out on the next leg of their journey. The forest around them was alive with the sounds of birds singing and leaves rustling in the gentle breeze. The air was filled with the earthy scent of pine and moss, and the sunlight filtered through the canopy, casting dappled shadows on the forest floor. Elara and Finn walked side by side, with Vixen the fox and Max the dog trotting alongside them, their eyes and ears alert for any signs of danger.

As they walked, Elara and Finn talked about the lessons they had learned from their encounter with Reynard, the Trickster Fox. They knew that trust was a valuable but fragile commodity, and they would need to be cautious as they continued their quest.

"We have to be careful who we trust," Elara said, her voice thoughtful. "Reynard helped us, but he also had his own agenda. We can't afford to be deceived again."

Finn nodded, his expression serious. "We need to trust our instincts and each other," he replied. "The forest will guide us if we listen to its whispers."

Their path led them through a dense thicket of trees, the undergrowth growing thicker and more tangled with each step. The whispers of the forest grew louder, urging them forward and filling their minds with a sense of urgency. It was as if the forest itself was guiding them toward something important.

After several hours of walking, they reached the edge of a small, secluded glade. The trees here were taller and more ancient, their branches forming a natural canopy that shaded the ground below. In the center of the glade stood a massive tree with silver bark and shimmering leaves. It was unlike any tree they had ever seen, and they knew immediately that it was special.

As they approached the tree, they noticed a narrow path leading away from the glade, winding through the trees and disappearing into the shadows. The whispers of the forest grew even louder, urging them to follow the path.

"This must be the way," Elara said, her voice filled with determination. "The forest wants us to go this way."

Finn nodded, and together they followed the path, Vixen and Max close at their heels. The path was narrow and winding, the trees closing in around them as they ventured deeper into the forest. The air grew cooler and more fragrant, filled with the scent of blooming flowers and fresh earth.

After what felt like hours of walking, they emerged into a small, hidden valley. The valley was unlike anything they had ever seen—a lush, verdant paradise filled with vibrant flowers, sparkling streams, and towering trees. In the center of the valley stood a village, its houses made of wood and stone, blending seamlessly with the natural surroundings.

As they approached the village, they were greeted by a group of forest spirits and magical creatures. The spirits were ethereal beings with glowing eyes and flowing hair, while the creatures included deer with silver antlers, birds with iridescent feathers, and rabbits with shimmering fur. The villagers watched them with a mixture of curiosity and caution, their eyes filled with wisdom and ancient knowledge.

"Welcome, travelers," said a tall, graceful spirit with silver hair and piercing blue eyes. "I am Lyra, the leader of this village. We have been expecting you."

Elara and Finn exchanged glances, surprised but relieved. They had felt the forest guiding them to this place, and it seemed that their arrival had been anticipated.

"We are Elara and Finn," Elara said, stepping forward. "We are on a quest to protect the Whispering Forest and uncover its secrets. The forest guided us here."

Lyra nodded, her expression serious. "We know of your quest," she said. "The whispers of the forest have told us of your bravery and determination. We are here to help you in any way we can."

She led them through the village, where they were greeted warmly by the other villagers. The houses were simple but beautifully crafted, adorned with flowers and vines that seemed to grow naturally from the walls. The villagers went about their daily tasks, tending to gardens, weaving cloth, and crafting tools and decorations.

As they walked, Lyra explained the history of the village. "This is Eldergrove, a hidden sanctuary for forest spirits and magical creatures," she said. "We have lived here for centuries, protecting the magic of the forest and maintaining the balance of nature. The Eldertree, the great tree you saw in the glade, is our guardian and source of wisdom."

She led them to the center of the village, where the Eldertree's branches extended over a large, open clearing. In the center of the clearing stood the Elder Tree, an ancient oak with a massive trunk and branches that reached high into the sky. Its bark was silver-gray, and its leaves shimmered with an ethereal light.

"The Elder Tree is the heart of our village," Lyra said, her voice filled with reverence. "It is a living repository of the forest's wisdom and magic. The tree speaks to us, guiding and protecting us. It has been waiting for you."

Elara and Finn approached the Elder Tree, their hearts filled with a sense of awe and reverence. They could feel the tree's powerful presence, a deep, resonant energy that seemed to pulse through the air. The whispers of the forest grew louder, filling their minds with a sense of calm and clarity.

"Welcome, Elara and Finn," a deep, melodic voice said. It seemed to come from the tree itself, resonating through the air and filling the clearing with its warmth. "I am the Elder Tree, guardian of Eldergrove and keeper of the forest's wisdom. I have been watching your journey and have much to tell you."

Elara and Finn listened intently as the Elder Tree began to speak, its voice filled with ancient knowledge and wisdom. The tree told them of the forest's history, its creation by the guardian spirits, and the many challenges it had faced over the centuries. It spoke of the darkness that threatened the forest, a malevolent force that sought to corrupt and destroy the magic of the land.

"The darkness is growing stronger," the Elder Tree said. "It seeks to consume the forest and all its inhabitants. You have been chosen to stand against this darkness, to protect the magic of the Whispering Forest and restore the balance of nature."

Elara and Finn exchanged determined glances. They had known their quest was important, but hearing it from the Elder Tree made the stakes even clearer.

"What must we do?" Elara asked, her voice steady and resolute.

"The Silver Leaf you carry is a powerful tool," the Elder Tree said. "It grants you the ability to communicate with the forest and understand its wisdom. But it is not enough. You must seek out the other guardian spirits and gather their knowledge and power. Only then will you be able to stand against the darkness and protect the forest."

The Elder Tree's branches swayed gently, as if nodding in agreement. "I will guide you to the first of these spirits," it said. "But be warned, the path ahead will be fraught with danger and deception. You must trust in yourselves and each other, and remain true to your hearts."

Elara and Finn nodded, their resolve strengthening. They had faced many challenges already, but they were ready to continue their quest and protect the Whispering Forest.

Before they set out on the next leg of their journey, Lyra introduced them to two villagers who would join them as allies. The first was a forest spirit named Rowan, a tall, strong figure with emerald-green eyes and hair like cascading ivy. Rowan was a skilled warrior and tracker, with a deep connection to the forest and its creatures.

The second ally was a magical creature named Thistle, a small, agile faun with curly brown hair and twinkling eyes. Thistle was quick and clever, with a talent for finding hidden paths and sensing danger. Together, Rowan and Thistle would provide invaluable support and guidance on their journey.

"We are honored to join you on your quest," Rowan said, his voice deep and steady. "The forest needs our protection, and we will do everything in our power to help."

Thistle grinned, her eyes sparkling with excitement. "This is going to be an adventure to remember," she said. "We'll face whatever challenges come our way and come out stronger on the other side."

With their new allies by their side, Elara and Finn felt a renewed sense of hope and determination. They knew that the journey ahead would be difficult, but they were ready to face it together. The whispers of the forest guided them, filling their hearts with wisdom and strength.

As they prepared to leave Eldergrove, the villagers gathered to see them off. Lyra handed Elara a small, intricately carved wooden box. "This is a gift from our village," she said. "Inside are seeds from the Eldertree. Plant them in times of need, and they will grow quickly, providing shelter and protection. Use them wisely."

Elara thanked Lyra, feeling a deep sense of gratitude for the village's support. With the box of seeds safely tucked into her pack, she and Finn set out with Rowan and Thistle, their hearts filled with resolve.

The path led them deeper into the forest, guided by the whispers and the wisdom of the Elder Tree. They encountered many challenges along the way, from treacherous terrain to cunning creatures, but with Rowan's strength and Thistle's agility, they overcame each obstacle.

One evening, as they set up camp by a small stream, Rowan shared more about his connection to the forest. "I was born in Eldergrove and have spent my entire life protecting the forest," he said. "The trees, the animals, the very earth itself—they are all part of me. I can feel their pain and joy, their fears and hopes. The darkness that threatens the forest is a powerful force, but together, we can stand against it."

Thistle nodded in agreement. "The forest has always been a place of magic and wonder," she said. "But it needs our help to stay that way. We have to be brave and clever, and trust in the wisdom of the trees."

Elara and Finn listened intently, their hearts filled with a deep sense of responsibility. They knew that their quest was not just about protecting the forest—it was about preserving a way of life, a connection to the magic and wisdom of nature.

As they continued their journey, they grew closer to Rowan and Thistle, their bonds of friendship and trust strengthening with each passing day. They faced many challenges and dangers, but with each trial, they grew stronger and more determined.

One particularly difficult challenge came in the form of a shadowy figure that appeared one evening as they set up camp. The figure was cloaked in darkness, its eyes glowing with an eerie light.

"Who are you?" Elara demanded, stepping forward with the Silver Leaf in hand.

The figure laughed, a cold, mocking sound that sent shivers down their spines. "I am a servant of the darkness," it said. "And I have come to claim the Silver Leaf for my master."

Finn stepped forward, his eyes blazing with determination. "You will not take it," he said. "We will protect the forest and its magic."

The shadowy figure lunged at them, but Rowan and Thistle stood their ground. Rowan's strength and Thistle's agility combined to create a formidable defense, and together, they repelled the attack.

As the figure retreated into the shadows, it hissed in anger. "This is not over," it snarled. "The darkness will consume you all."

Elara and Finn watched as the figure disappeared, their hearts pounding with a mixture of fear and determination. They knew that the darkness was a formidable enemy, but they were ready to face it head-on.

"We have to stay strong," Elara said, her voice steady. "The forest is counting on us."

Finn nodded, his eyes filled with resolve. "We won't let the darkness win," he said. "We'll protect the Whispering Forest with everything we have."

With Rowan and Thistle by their side, they continued their journey, guided by the whispers and the wisdom of the forest. They encountered many more challenges, each one testing their courage, intelligence, and bond with the land.

As they traveled, they learned more about the forest's history and the guardian spirits that protected it. The Elder Tree had told them of the first guardian spirit they needed to seek out—an ancient being known as the Spirit of the Waterfall.

"The Spirit of the Waterfall is a powerful guardian," the Elder Tree had said. "She resides in a hidden grotto behind the great waterfall, deep within the forest. She holds the knowledge of the water's magic and can provide valuable guidance and protection. But be warned, she is cautious and will only reveal herself to those who prove their worthiness."

Elara and Finn knew that finding the Spirit of the Waterfall would be a crucial step in their quest. With Rowan and Thistle's help, they navigated the treacherous terrain, crossing rivers and climbing steep cliffs as they made their way to the waterfall.

As they approached the waterfall, they could hear the thunderous roar of the water cascading down the rocks. The air was filled with mist, and the ground was slick with moisture. They knew that reaching the hidden grotto would be difficult, but they were determined to succeed.

"We have to find a way behind the waterfall," Elara said, her voice determined. "The Spirit of the Waterfall is waiting for us."

Rowan nodded, his eyes scanning the rocky cliffs for a way through. "There must be a hidden path," he said. "We just have to find it."

Thistle darted ahead, her nimble form easily navigating the slippery rocks. "I think I see something," she called out, pointing to a narrow ledge that seemed to lead behind the waterfall.

Elara and Finn followed Thistle, carefully making their way across the ledge. The roar of the waterfall grew louder, and the mist made it difficult to see, but they pressed on, determined to reach the hidden grotto.

As they rounded the last bend, they found themselves in a small, secluded grotto. The air was cool and filled with the sound of the waterfall, and the walls of the grotto were covered in glowing moss and delicate ferns. In the center of the grotto stood a tall, graceful figure with flowing silver hair and eyes like sparkling water.

"Welcome, travelers," the figure said, her voice like the gentle rush of a stream. "I am the Spirit of the Waterfall. The forest has told me of your quest, and I have been waiting for you."

Elara and Finn stepped forward, their hearts filled with a sense of awe and reverence. They could feel the spirit's powerful presence, a deep, resonant energy that seemed to pulse through the air.

"We are honored to meet you," Elara said, her voice steady. "We are on a quest to protect the Whispering Forest and uncover its secrets. The Elder Tree sent us to seek your guidance."

The Spirit of the Waterfall nodded, her eyes filled with wisdom and ancient knowledge. "I can see the determination in your hearts," she said. "But the path ahead is fraught with danger. The darkness that threatens the forest is a powerful force, and it will stop at nothing to achieve its goals."

She paused, her gaze intense. "To stand against the darkness, you must gather the knowledge and power of the guardian spirits. I will share with you the magic of the water and the wisdom of the forest, but you must prove your worthiness."

Elara and Finn nodded, ready to face whatever challenge lay ahead. "We are ready," Finn said, his voice filled with resolve. "We will do whatever it takes to protect the forest."

The Spirit of the Waterfall smiled, her eyes twinkling with approval. "Very well," she said. "Your first task is to retrieve a sacred stone from the depths of the waterfall. It is a powerful artifact that holds the essence of the water's magic. But be warned, the path to the stone is treacherous, and only the bravest and most determined will succeed."

Elara and Finn exchanged determined glances, their hearts filled with resolve. With Rowan and Thistle by their side, they knew they could overcome any challenge.

The Spirit of the Waterfall led them to the edge of the grotto, where a narrow path wound down to the base of the waterfall. The path was slick with moisture, and the roar of the water was deafening, but they pressed on, determined to retrieve the sacred stone.

As they descended the path, they encountered several obstacles, from slippery rocks to rushing currents. Each obstacle tested their courage and determination, but with Rowan's strength and Thistle's agility, they overcame each challenge.

At the base of the waterfall, they found a small, hidden pool. The water was crystal clear, and at the bottom of the pool lay the sacred stone, glowing with an ethereal light.

Elara and Finn took a deep breath and dove into the pool, the cold water shocking their senses. They swam down to the bottom, their hands reaching out to grasp the stone. As they touched it, they felt a surge of energy, a deep, resonant magic that filled their hearts and minds.

With the sacred stone in hand, they swam back to the surface, their hearts pounding with triumph. They had proven their worthiness and retrieved the artifact.

The Spirit of the Waterfall awaited them at the edge of the pool, her eyes filled with approval. "You have done well," she said. "The sacred stone holds the essence of the water's magic. With it, you will be able to harness the power of the water and protect the forest."

She placed her hands over the stone, and a soft, blue light enveloped it. "This stone is a powerful tool, but it is also a responsibility. Use it wisely and with respect, for the magic of the water is both gentle and fierce."

Elara and Finn nodded, their hearts filled with gratitude and determination. With the sacred stone in their possession, they felt a renewed sense of hope and strength.

The Spirit of the Waterfall smiled, her eyes twinkling with wisdom. "Your journey is far from over," she said. "But with the knowledge and power of the guardian spirits, you will be able to stand against the darkness and protect the Whispering Forest. Remember the lessons you have learned and trust in yourselves and each other."

With those words of wisdom, the Spirit of the Waterfall disappeared into the mist, leaving Elara and Finn with a sense of purpose and resolve. They had gained valuable allies and powerful tools, and they were ready to continue their quest.

As they made their way back to the village of Eldergrove, the whispers of the forest guided them, filling their hearts with wisdom and strength. They knew that their journey would be difficult, but they were ready to face it together, with the knowledge and power of the guardian spirits by their side.

With Rowan and Thistle as their allies, and the sacred stone in their possession, Elara and Finn felt a renewed sense of hope and determination. They would protect the Whispering Forest and ensure that its magic and wisdom would endure

for generations to come. Together, they would stand against the darkness and preserve the magic of the land they loved.

As they approached Eldergrove, they were greeted warmly by the villagers, who had been eagerly awaiting their return. Lyra, the leader of the village, welcomed them with open arms, her eyes filled with pride and relief.

"You have done well," Lyra said, her voice filled with warmth. "The forest has told us of your bravery and determination. You have proven yourselves worthy of the guardian spirits' knowledge and power. We are honored to have you as our allies."

Elara and Finn thanked Lyra and the villagers for their support, their hearts filled with gratitude and resolve. They knew that their quest was far from over, but with the knowledge and power they had gained, they felt ready to face whatever challenges lay ahead.

As they rested and prepared for the next leg of their journey, they reflected on the lessons they had learned and the bonds they had formed. They had faced many challenges and dangers, but they had also gained valuable allies and powerful tools. They knew that the road ahead would be difficult, but they were ready to face it together, with the wisdom and strength of the Whispering Forest guiding them.

Their adventure was far from over, but they faced it with courage and determination. The hidden village of Eldergrove had given them new allies and powerful tools, and they were stronger for it. Together, they would protect the Whispering Forest and ensure that its magic and wisdom would endure for generations to come.

# Chapter 6: The Night of the Dancing Lights

The Whispering Forest was known for its beauty and magic, but there was one phenomenon that surpassed all others: the Dancing Lights. This mesmerizing event occurred only once a decade, transforming the forest into a shimmering wonderland of ethereal light. For centuries, the Dancing Lights had been a source of awe and mystery, and many believed they held a deep connection to the forest's ancient magic. As Elara, Finn, Rowan, and Thistle continued their quest, they eagerly anticipated the arrival of the Dancing Lights, knowing that they held the key to the next step of their journey.

The night of the Dancing Lights was approaching, and the forest seemed to hum with anticipation. The air was thick with the scent of pine and blooming flowers, and the trees rustled softly as if whispering secrets to each other. The whispers of the forest had guided Elara and her companions to a secluded glade, a place of profound tranquility and beauty. The glade was surrounded by ancient trees, their branches forming a natural canopy that filtered the moonlight into a soft, silvery glow.

As the sun began to set, casting long shadows across the glade, Elara and Finn set up camp, their hearts filled with excitement and wonder. Rowan and Thistle gathered firewood and prepared a simple meal, their movements sure and efficient. Vixen and Max trotted around the glade, their senses alert for any signs of danger.

"The Dancing Lights will appear tonight," Rowan said, his deep voice filled with reverence. "It is a rare and wondrous event, one that few have the privilege to witness. The lights are a manifestation of the forest's magic, a reminder of its ancient power and wisdom."

Thistle nodded, her eyes sparkling with excitement. "The lights are said to reveal hidden truths and offer guidance to those who seek it," she added. "We must be ready to embrace their magic and learn from their wisdom."

As darkness fell, the glade was bathed in the soft glow of the moonlight. The air grew cooler, and the sounds of the forest seemed to fade into a hushed silence. Elara and Finn sat by the campfire, their eyes fixed on the sky, waiting for the first sign of the Dancing Lights.

Hours passed, and the anticipation grew. Just as Elara was beginning to wonder if the lights would appear, a faint shimmer of light flickered at the edge of the glade. She gasped, her heart pounding with excitement.

"Look!" she whispered, pointing to the shimmering light.

Finn followed her gaze, his eyes widening with awe. "It's starting," he said, his voice barely audible.

The shimmering light grew brighter, spreading across the sky like a wave of luminescent magic. The trees seemed to come alive with a soft, ethereal glow, their leaves shimmering with an otherworldly light. The air was filled with a gentle, melodic hum, a symphony of sound that resonated with the very essence of the forest.

As the light grew brighter, it began to dance across the sky, forming intricate patterns and shapes. Swirls of light twisted and turned, creating a mesmerizing display of colors and movement. It was as if the stars themselves had descended to the earth, joining in a celestial dance that captivated all who watched.

Elara and Finn watched in awe, their hearts filled with wonder. The Dancing Lights were unlike anything they had ever seen, a breathtaking display of magic and beauty that seemed to transcend the boundaries of reality.

"The Dancing Lights are a manifestation of the forest's ancient magic," Rowan said, his voice filled with reverence. "They are a reminder of the power and wisdom that reside within the forest, a connection to the past and a guide to the future."

Thistle nodded, her eyes fixed on the dancing lights. "The lights are said to reveal hidden truths and offer guidance to those who seek it," she added. "We must be ready to embrace their magic and learn from their wisdom."

As the lights continued to dance across the sky, a sense of calm and clarity filled the glade. The whispers of the forest grew louder, their voices blending with the melodic hum of the lights. Elara felt a deep connection to the forest, a bond that seemed to transcend time and space.

"We need to listen to the whispers and let them guide us," Elara said, her voice steady and determined. "The Dancing Lights hold the key to the next step of our journey."

Finn nodded, his eyes filled with resolve. "We must be open to the magic and wisdom of the lights," he said. "They will show us the way."

As they watched the Dancing Lights, the patterns and shapes began to shift, forming a series of symbols and images. It was as if the lights were trying to communicate with them, offering clues and guidance.

"The lights are speaking to us," Rowan said, his voice filled with wonder. "We must pay close attention and decipher their message."

Elara, Finn, Rowan, and Thistle focused intently on the dancing lights, their minds attuned to the whispers and the magic of the forest. The symbols and images seemed to flow together, creating a tapestry of light and color that told a story.

"The lights are revealing a riddle," Thistle said, her eyes sparkling with excitement. "We must solve it to proceed on our journey."

Elara and Finn exchanged determined glances, ready to face the challenge. They knew that the riddle held the key to the next step of their quest, and they were determined to decipher its meaning.

The symbols and images continued to shift and change, forming a series of clues that seemed to blend together in a harmonious dance. The lights created a beautiful tapestry of glowing patterns, and as Elara and her companions watched, the shapes began to form words in a language they could almost understand. They knew they had to focus their minds and hearts to decipher the riddle.

"The riddle is part of the forest's magic," Rowan said, his voice filled with reverence. "We must be patient and listen with our hearts to understand its meaning."

Thistle nodded, her eyes fixed on the glowing symbols. "The lights are guiding us," she said. "We need to trust in their wisdom and let them show us the way."

As the symbols continued to shift and change, Elara and Finn felt a sense of clarity and understanding. The lights seemed to weave a story, revealing a series of clues that formed a coherent riddle. The words began to take shape, and they read:

"In the heart of the ancient wood,
Where time stands still and shadows brood,
Seek the place where light and dark meet,
Where secrets whisper and spirits greet.
Find the tree with silver leaves,
That sways in the moonlit breeze,
Beneath its boughs, the answer lies,
In the echoes of forgotten cries.
Speak the words that hearts do hold,
Unlock the door to treasures old,
For those who seek with pure intent,
Shall find the path that fate has sent."

Elara and Finn repeated the riddle, their minds working to decipher its meaning. They knew that the clues held the key to the next step of their journey, and they were determined to uncover the secrets hidden within the words.

"The heart of the ancient wood," Elara said thoughtfully. "Where time stands still and shadows brood. That must be a specific place in the forest."

Rowan nodded in agreement. "The place where light and dark meet could refer to a clearing or a glade," he said. "And the tree with silver leaves sounds like a specific tree we need to find."

Thistle's eyes sparkled with excitement. "The answer lies beneath its boughs," she said. "We need to find this tree and speak the words that our hearts hold. The riddle will guide us to the next step of our quest."

As they continued to ponder the riddle, the Dancing Lights began to fade, their shimmering glow gradually dimming until the forest was once again bathed in the soft light of the moon. The glade was filled with a sense of calm and tranquility, as if the magic of the lights had left a lasting imprint on the land.

"We need to find the tree with silver leaves," Finn said, his voice filled with determination. "That's where the answer to the riddle lies."

Elara nodded, her resolve strengthening. "The lights have shown us the way," she said. "We must follow their guidance and trust in the wisdom of the forest."

With renewed determination, Elara, Finn, Rowan, and Thistle set out to find the tree with silver leaves. The whispers of the forest guided them, their voices filled with encouragement and support. They knew that the journey ahead would be challenging, but they were ready to face whatever obstacles lay in their path.

As they ventured deeper into the heart of the forest, they encountered a series of challenges and trials. They navigated treacherous terrain, crossed rushing rivers, and faced cunning creatures that sought to impede their progress. But with each trial, their bond grew stronger, and their determination never wavered.

One particularly difficult challenge came in the form of a dense, shadowy thicket that seemed to block their path. The thicket was filled with twisted vines and thorny bushes, creating a nearly impenetrable barrier. The whispers of the forest urged them to find a way through, but the path seemed impossible.

"We need to find a way around this thicket," Elara said, her voice filled with determination. "The tree with silver leaves must be on the other side."

Rowan examined the thicket, his eyes scanning for any sign of a hidden path. "There must be a way through," he said. "We just need to find it."

Thistle darted ahead, her nimble form easily navigating the tangled vines. "I think I see something," she called out, pointing to a narrow gap in the thicket.

Elara and Finn followed Thistle, carefully making their way through the narrow gap. The vines scratched at their skin and clothing, but they pressed on, determined to reach the other side. Vixen and Max stayed close, their senses alert for any signs of danger.

After what felt like hours of struggling through the thicket, they finally emerged into a small clearing. The clearing was bathed in the soft glow of the moonlight, and in the center stood a tall, ancient tree with silver leaves that shimmered in the breeze. The tree swayed gently, its branches forming a natural canopy that cast dappled shadows on the ground.

"This must be the tree," Finn said, his voice filled with awe. "The tree with silver leaves."

Elara nodded, her heart pounding with excitement. "The answer to the riddle lies beneath its boughs," she said. "We need to speak the words that our hearts hold."

As they approached the tree, they felt a deep, resonant energy emanating from its trunk and branches. The whispers of the forest grew louder, filling their minds with a sense of calm and clarity. They knew that they were in the right place, and that the tree held the key to the next step of their journey.

Elara stepped forward, her hand gently touching the trunk of the tree. She closed her eyes and took a deep breath, focusing on the words that her heart held.

"Ancient tree, guardian of the forest's wisdom," she began, her voice steady and clear. "We seek the guidance and protection of the forest. We have come with pure intent and open hearts. Show us the path that fate has sent."

As Elara spoke the words, the tree's silver leaves began to shimmer and glow with an ethereal light. The ground beneath their feet seemed to hum with energy, and a soft, melodic voice filled the air.

"You have spoken the words of truth and purity," the voice said. "The path to the next step of your journey lies before you. Follow the light and trust in the wisdom of the forest."

A beam of light appeared at the base of the tree, forming a glowing path that led deeper into the forest. Elara, Finn, Rowan, and Thistle followed the path, their hearts filled with hope and determination. They knew that the tree with silver leaves had shown them the way, and that the forest's magic was guiding them.

As they walked along the glowing path, they felt a deep sense of connection to the forest and its ancient magic. The whispers of the forest filled their minds with wisdom and strength, encouraging them to continue their quest.

The path led them to a small, hidden glade, where a group of forest spirits and magical creatures awaited them. The spirits were ethereal beings with glowing eyes and flowing hair, while the creatures included deer with silver antlers, birds with iridescent feathers, and rabbits with shimmering fur.

"Welcome, travelers," said a tall, graceful spirit with silver hair and piercing blue eyes. "I am Aeliana, the guardian of this glade. The forest has told us of your bravery and determination. We are here to help you in any way we can."

Elara and Finn exchanged grateful glances, their hearts filled with gratitude for the forest's support. They knew that their quest was far from over, but with the help of the forest spirits and magical creatures, they felt ready to face whatever challenges lay ahead.

"We are honored to meet you," Elara said, her voice steady and determined. "We are on a quest to protect the Whispering Forest and uncover its secrets. The tree with silver leaves guided us here."

Aeliana nodded, her expression serious and compassionate. "The forest's magic is strong, and its wisdom is deep," she said. "You have proven yourselves worthy of its guidance. But the darkness that threatens the forest is a powerful force, and it will stop at nothing to achieve its goals. You must gather the knowledge and power of the guardian spirits to stand against it."

Thistle's eyes sparkled with excitement. "We will do whatever it takes to protect the forest," she said. "We are ready to face the challenges ahead."

Aeliana smiled, her eyes twinkling with approval. "Your determination and courage are commendable," she said. "The next step of your journey will take you to the Realm of Shadows, where the guardian spirit known as the Keeper of the Night resides. She holds the knowledge of the shadows and the power to control the darkness. You must seek her out and gain her guidance and protection."

Elara and Finn nodded, their resolve strengthening. They knew that the journey ahead would be difficult, but they were ready to face it together.

"We will find the Keeper of the Night," Elara said, her voice filled with determination. "And we will protect the Whispering Forest with everything we have."

With renewed hope and strength, Elara, Finn, Rowan, and Thistle set out on the next leg of their journey, guided by the whispers and the wisdom of the forest. They knew that the path ahead would be fraught with danger and deception, but they were ready to face whatever obstacles lay in their path.

As they ventured deeper into the forest, they encountered a series of trials and challenges that tested their courage, intelligence, and bond with the land. They navigated treacherous terrain, crossed rushing rivers, and faced cunning creatures that sought to impede their progress. But with each trial, their bond grew stronger, and their determination never wavered.

One particularly difficult challenge came in the form of a dense, shadowy forest known as the Darkwood. The Darkwood was filled with twisted trees and thick undergrowth, creating a nearly impenetrable barrier. The whispers of the forest urged them to find a way through, but the path seemed impossible.

"We need to find a way through the Darkwood," Finn said, his voice filled with determination. "The Keeper of the Night must be on the other side."

Rowan examined the Darkwood, his eyes scanning for any sign of a hidden path. "There must be a way through," he said. "We just need to find it."

Thistle darted ahead, her nimble form easily navigating the tangled undergrowth. "I think I see something," she called out, pointing to a narrow gap in the trees.

Elara and Finn followed Thistle, carefully making their way through the narrow gap. The undergrowth scratched at their skin and clothing, but they pressed on, determined to reach the other side. Vixen and Max stayed close, their senses alert for any signs of danger.

After what felt like hours of struggling through the Darkwood, they finally emerged into a small clearing. The clearing was bathed in the soft glow of the moonlight, and in the center stood a tall, ancient tree with dark, shadowy leaves that seemed to absorb the light.

"This must be the tree," Elara said, her voice filled with awe. "The tree that marks the entrance to the Realm of Shadows."

Finn nodded, his heart pounding with excitement. "The Keeper of the Night must be near," he said. "We need to find her and seek her guidance."

As they approached the tree, they felt a deep, resonant energy emanating from its trunk and branches. The whispers of the forest grew louder, filling their minds with a sense of calm and clarity. They knew that they were in the right place, and that the tree held the key to the next step of their journey.

Elara stepped forward, her hand gently touching the trunk of the tree. She closed her eyes and took a deep breath, focusing on the words that her heart held.

"Ancient tree, guardian of the Realm of Shadows," she began, her voice steady and clear. "We seek the guidance and protection of the Keeper of the Night. We have come with pure intent and open hearts. Show us the path that fate has sent."

As Elara spoke the words, the tree's shadowy leaves began to shimmer and glow with an ethereal light. The ground beneath their feet seemed to hum with energy, and a soft, melodic voice filled the air.

"You have spoken the words of truth and purity," the voice said. "The path to the Keeper of the Night lies before you. Follow the light and trust in the wisdom of the forest."

A beam of light appeared at the base of the tree, forming a glowing path that led deeper into the Realm of Shadows. Elara, Finn, Rowan, and Thistle followed the path, their hearts filled with hope and determination. They knew that the tree had shown them the way, and that the forest's magic was guiding them.

As they walked along the glowing path, they felt a deep sense of connection to the forest and its ancient magic. The whispers of the forest filled their minds with wisdom and strength, encouraging them to continue their quest.

The path led them to a small, hidden glade, where the Keeper of the Night awaited them. The Keeper was a tall, graceful figure with flowing black hair and eyes like the night sky. She exuded an aura of power and mystery, and her presence filled the glade with a sense of calm and tranquility.

"Welcome, travelers," the Keeper of the Night said, her voice like the gentle rustle of leaves in the wind. "I am the Keeper of the Night, guardian of the Realm of Shadows. The forest has told me of your bravery and determination. I am here to help you in any way I can."

Elara and Finn stepped forward, their hearts filled with gratitude and resolve. They knew that the Keeper of the Night held the key to the next step of their journey, and they were determined to seek her guidance.

"We are honored to meet you," Elara said, her voice steady and determined. "We are on a quest to protect the Whispering Forest and uncover its secrets. The tree with silver leaves guided us here."

The Keeper of the Night nodded, her expression serious and compassionate. "The forest's magic is strong, and its wisdom is deep," she said. "You have proven yourselves worthy of its guidance. But the darkness that threatens the forest is a powerful force, and it will stop at nothing to achieve its goals. You must gather the knowledge and power of the guardian spirits to stand against it."

Thistle's eyes sparkled with excitement. "We will do whatever it takes to protect the forest," she said. "We are ready to face the challenges ahead."

The Keeper of the Night smiled, her eyes twinkling with approval. "Your determination and courage are commendable," she said. "The next step of your journey will take you to the Cavern of Echoes, where the guardian spirit known as the Voice of the Mountain resides. She holds the knowledge of the earth and the power to shape the land. You must seek her out and gain her guidance and protection."

Elara and Finn nodded, their resolve strengthening. They knew that the journey ahead would be difficult, but they were ready to face it together.

"We will find the Voice of the Mountain," Elara said, her voice filled with determination. "And we will protect the Whispering Forest with everything we have."

With renewed hope and strength, Elara, Finn, Rowan, and Thistle set out on the next leg of their journey, guided by the whispers and the wisdom of the forest. They knew that the path ahead would be fraught with danger and deception, but they were ready to face whatever obstacles lay in their path.

As they ventured deeper into the forest, they encountered a series of trials and challenges that tested their courage, intelligence, and bond with the land. They navigated treacherous terrain, crossed rushing rivers, and faced cunning creatures that sought to impede their progress. But with each trial, their bond grew stronger, and their determination never wavered.

Their adventure was far from over, but they faced it with courage and determination. The Night of the Dancing Lights had given them new allies and powerful tools, and they were stronger for it. Together, they would protect the Whispering Forest and ensure that its magic and wisdom would endure for generations to come.

# Chapter 7: The Witch of the Wildwood

The Whispering Forest held many secrets, but none as enigmatic as the Witch of the Wildwood. As Elara, Finn, Rowan, and Thistle continued their quest to protect the forest, they knew that confronting this powerful witch was inevitable. The Witch of the Wildwood was said to guard the entrance to the deepest part of the forest, a place where ancient magic and untold dangers resided. To continue their journey, they would have to overcome her trials and earn her respect.

The whispers of the forest guided them through dense thickets and along winding paths, leading them closer to the witch's domain. The air grew cooler and filled with the scent of damp earth and blooming flowers. The trees around them seemed to grow taller and more imposing, their branches forming a dense canopy that blocked out much of the sunlight.

As they ventured deeper into the forest, Elara and Finn felt a growing sense of anticipation and apprehension. They knew that the Witch of the Wildwood was a formidable adversary, but they were determined to face her and prove their worth.

"We're getting close," Rowan said, his deep voice cutting through the silence. "The witch's domain lies just ahead. We must be prepared for anything."

Thistle nodded, her eyes scanning the forest around them. "The Witch of the Wildwood is known for her cunning and power," she said. "We need to stay alert and trust in each other."

Elara and Finn exchanged determined glances, their resolve strengthening. They had faced many challenges on their journey, and they knew that this confrontation would be one of the most difficult yet. But they were ready to face it together, with the wisdom and strength of the forest guiding them.

As they approached a dense thicket of ancient trees, the whispers of the forest grew louder, urging them forward. The path narrowed, and the air grew thick with an otherworldly energy. The trees seemed to close in around them, their branches forming a natural barrier that blocked their way.

"This must be the entrance to the witch's domain," Finn said, his voice filled with determination. "We need to find a way through."

Rowan examined the barrier of trees, his eyes scanning for any sign of a hidden path. "There must be a way to open the barrier," he said. "The witch's magic is strong, but we can find a way through."

Thistle darted ahead, her nimble form easily navigating the twisted branches. "I think I see something," she called out, pointing to a faint glow emanating from the base of one of the trees.

Elara and Finn followed Thistle, carefully making their way through the tangled branches. As they reached the source of the glow, they found a small, intricately carved stone set into the ground. The stone was covered in ancient runes that pulsed with a soft, blue light.

"This stone must be the key to opening the barrier," Elara said, her voice filled with wonder. "We need to decipher the runes and unlock its magic."

Rowan examined the runes, his eyes narrowing in concentration. "The runes are written in an ancient language," he said. "We need to find the right words to activate the stone's magic."

Thistle's eyes sparkled with excitement. "I recognize some of these runes," she said. "They speak of balance and harmony, of light and dark. We need to speak the words of balance to unlock the barrier."

Elara and Finn nodded, their hearts pounding with anticipation. They joined hands and focused their minds, drawing on the wisdom and strength of the forest.

"Light and dark, balance and harmony," Elara began, her voice steady and clear. "We seek the path to deeper wisdom, to the heart of the ancient forest. Guide us, guardian of the Wildwood, and show us the way."

As Elara spoke the words, the stone began to glow more brightly, and the runes pulsed with a rhythmic light. The ground beneath their feet seemed to hum with energy, and a soft, melodic voice filled the air.

"You have spoken the words of balance and harmony," the voice said. "The path to the Witch of the Wildwood lies before you. Enter and face her trials with courage and determination."

The barrier of trees began to part, creating a narrow passage that led deeper into the forest. Elara, Finn, Rowan, and Thistle stepped forward, their hearts filled with resolve. They knew that the witch's trials would be difficult, but they were ready to face whatever challenges lay ahead.

As they ventured deeper into the witch's domain, the forest grew darker and more foreboding. The trees seemed to whisper warnings, and the air was thick with an eerie silence. They knew that the witch was watching them, her presence a constant, unseen force.

After several hours of walking, they reached a small clearing. In the center of the clearing stood a tall, imposing figure draped in dark, flowing robes. Her hair was long and black, and her eyes glowed with an otherworldly light. She exuded an aura of power and mystery, and her presence filled the clearing with a sense of tension and anticipation.

"Welcome, travelers," the witch said, her voice like the rustle of leaves in the wind. "I am Morgana, the Witch of the Wildwood. I have been expecting you."

Elara and Finn stepped forward, their hearts filled with a mixture of fear and determination. They knew that this confrontation would be one of the most challenging yet, but they were ready to face it together.

"We seek your guidance and protection," Elara said, her voice steady. "We are on a quest to protect the Whispering Forest and uncover its secrets. We need to pass through your domain to continue our journey."

Morgana's eyes narrowed, and a faint smile played at the corners of her lips. "Many have come seeking my guidance and protection," she said. "But few have proven themselves worthy. You must face my trials and earn my respect before I will grant you passage."

Finn stepped forward, his eyes blazing with determination. "We are ready to face your trials," he said. "We will do whatever it takes to protect the forest."

Morgana's smile widened, and she raised her hands, casting a series of intricate spells. The air around them shimmered with magic, and the clearing was transformed into a labyrinth of twisting paths and hidden dangers.

"Your first trial is a test of courage and resolve," Morgana said. "You must navigate this labyrinth and reach the heart of the Wildwood. Only then will you prove yourselves worthy of my guidance."

Elara, Finn, Rowan, and Thistle nodded, their hearts filled with determination. They knew that the labyrinth would be filled with challenges, but they were ready to face whatever obstacles lay ahead.

As they entered the labyrinth, the paths twisted and turned, creating a disorienting maze of trees and shadows. The air was thick with an otherworldly energy, and the whispers of the forest seemed to fade into the background.

"We need to stay together and trust in each other," Elara said, her voice steady. "The labyrinth is designed to test our courage and resolve. We must not lose our way."

Rowan nodded, his eyes scanning the paths for any sign of danger. "We need to keep moving and stay focused," he said. "The labyrinth is filled with traps and illusions. We must be vigilant."

Thistle darted ahead, her nimble form easily navigating the twisting paths. "I can sense the magic of the labyrinth," she said. "We need to follow the path of light. It will lead us to the heart of the Wildwood."

Elara and Finn followed Thistle, carefully making their way through the labyrinth. The paths were filled with hidden traps and illusions, designed to confuse and deceive them. They encountered shadowy figures that sought to block their way, but they stood their ground and pressed on, determined to reach the heart of the Wildwood.

As they ventured deeper into the labyrinth, they felt a growing sense of tension and anticipation. The paths grew darker and more twisted, and the air was filled with an eerie silence. They knew that they were nearing the heart of the Wildwood, and that the most difficult part of the trial lay ahead.

After what felt like hours of navigating the labyrinth, they reached a small clearing. In the center of the clearing stood a tall, ancient tree with dark, shadowy leaves that seemed to absorb the light. The tree swayed gently, its branches forming a natural canopy that cast dappled shadows on the ground.

"This must be the heart of the Wildwood," Finn said, his voice filled with awe. "We need to prove our worthiness to Morgana."

As they approached the tree, they felt a deep, resonant energy emanating from its trunk and branches. The whispers of the forest grew louder, filling their minds with a sense of calm and clarity. They knew that they were in the right place, and that the tree held the key to the next step of their journey.

Morgana appeared before them, her eyes glowing with an otherworldly light. "You have reached the heart of the Wildwood," she said. "But your trials are not yet over. You must face one final test to prove your worthiness."

She raised her hands, casting a powerful spell that enveloped the clearing in a shimmering light. The ground beneath their feet seemed to hum with energy, and a series of ancient runes appeared on the trunk of the tree.

"This is a test of wisdom and insight," Morgana said. "You must decipher the runes and unlock the magic of the tree. Only then will you earn my respect and receive the artifact you seek."

Elara, Finn, Rowan, and Thistle examined the runes, their minds working to decipher their meaning. The runes were written in an ancient language, and they knew that they held the key to unlocking the tree's magic.

"The runes speak of balance and harmony, of light and dark," Elara said thoughtfully. "We need to find the right words to activate the tree's magic."

Rowan nodded, his eyes scanning the runes for any clues. "The tree is a guardian of the forest's wisdom," he said. "We need to speak the words of truth and purity to unlock its magic."

Thistle's eyes sparkled with excitement. "I recognize some of these runes," she said. "They speak of the ancient magic of the forest, of the balance between light and dark. We need to trust in the wisdom of the forest and speak the words that our hearts hold."

Elara and Finn joined hands, focusing their minds and hearts on the runes. They drew on the wisdom and strength of the forest, speaking the words that their hearts held.

"Ancient tree, guardian of the Wildwood's wisdom," Elara began, her voice steady and clear. "We seek the guidance and protection of the forest. We have come with pure intent and open hearts. Show us the path that fate has sent."

As Elara spoke the words, the runes began to glow with a soft, blue light. The ground beneath their feet seemed to hum with energy, and the tree's branches swayed gently, as if acknowledging their words.

"You have spoken the words of truth and purity," Morgana said, her voice filled with approval. "You have proven yourselves worthy of my respect. I will grant you the artifact you seek."

She raised her hands, casting a spell that caused the tree to shimmer and glow with an ethereal light. A small, intricately carved wooden box appeared at the base of the tree, its surface covered in ancient runes.

"This box contains a magical artifact that will aid you on your quest," Morgana said. "It holds the essence of the Wildwood's magic, a powerful tool that will help you protect the forest and stand against the darkness. Use it wisely and with respect."

Elara and Finn stepped forward, their hearts filled with gratitude and determination. They carefully picked up the wooden box, feeling its smooth surface and the warmth of its magic.

"Thank you, Morgana," Elara said, her voice filled with gratitude. "We will use the artifact to protect the forest and continue our quest."

Morgana smiled, her eyes twinkling with approval. "You have earned my respect and my guidance," she said. "The path to the deeper part of the forest lies before you. Follow the whispers and trust in the wisdom of the forest. You are ready to face whatever challenges lie ahead."

With renewed hope and strength, Elara, Finn, Rowan, and Thistle set out on the next leg of their journey, guided by the whispers and the wisdom of the forest. They knew that the path ahead would be fraught with danger and deception, but they were ready to face whatever obstacles lay in their path.

As they ventured deeper into the forest, they encountered a series of trials and challenges that tested their courage, intelligence, and bond with the land. They navigated treacherous terrain, crossed rushing rivers, and faced cunning creatures that sought to impede their progress. But with each trial, their bond grew stronger, and their determination never wavered.

One particularly difficult challenge came in the form of a dense, shadowy forest known as the Darkwood. The Darkwood was filled with twisted trees and thick undergrowth, creating a nearly impenetrable barrier. The whispers of the forest urged them to find a way through, but the path seemed impossible.

"We need to find a way through the Darkwood," Finn said, his voice filled with determination. "The deeper part of the forest must be on the other side."

Rowan examined the Darkwood, his eyes scanning for any sign of a hidden path. "There must be a way through," he said. "We just need to find it."

Thistle darted ahead, her nimble form easily navigating the tangled undergrowth. "I think I see something," she called out, pointing to a narrow gap in the trees.

Elara and Finn followed Thistle, carefully making their way through the narrow gap. The undergrowth scratched at their skin and clothing, but they pressed on, determined to reach the other side. Vixen and Max stayed close, their senses alert for any signs of danger.

After what felt like hours of struggling through the Darkwood, they finally emerged into a small clearing. The clearing was bathed in the soft glow of the moonlight, and in the center stood a tall, ancient tree with dark, shadowy leaves that seemed to absorb the light.

"This must be the tree," Elara said, her voice filled with awe. "The tree that marks the entrance to the deeper part of the forest."

Finn nodded, his heart pounding with excitement. "We need to find a way to unlock its magic," he said. "The whispers of the forest will guide us."

As they approached the tree, they felt a deep, resonant energy emanating from its trunk and branches. The whispers of the forest grew louder, filling their minds with a sense of calm and clarity. They knew that they were in the right place, and that the tree held the key to the next step of their journey.

Elara stepped forward, her hand gently touching the trunk of the tree. She closed her eyes and took a deep breath, focusing on the words that her heart held.

"Ancient tree, guardian of the deeper forest," she began, her voice steady and clear. "We seek the guidance and protection of the forest. We have come with pure intent and open hearts. Show us the path that fate has sent."

As Elara spoke the words, the tree's shadowy leaves began to shimmer and glow with an ethereal light. The ground beneath their feet seemed to hum with energy, and a soft, melodic voice filled the air.

"You have spoken the words of truth and purity," the voice said. "The path to the deeper part of the forest lies before you. Follow the light and trust in the wisdom of the forest."

A beam of light appeared at the base of the tree, forming a glowing path that led deeper into the forest. Elara, Finn, Rowan, and Thistle followed the path, their hearts filled with hope and determination. They knew that the tree had shown them the way, and that the forest's magic was guiding them.

As they walked along the glowing path, they felt a deep sense of connection to the forest and its ancient magic. The whispers of the forest filled their minds with wisdom and strength, encouraging them to continue their quest.

The path led them to a small, hidden glade, where the next part of their journey awaited them. They knew that the challenges ahead would be difficult, but with the wisdom and strength of the forest guiding them, they felt ready to face whatever obstacles lay in their path.

Their adventure was far from over, but they faced it with courage and determination. The encounter with the Witch of the Wildwood had given them new allies and powerful tools, and they were stronger for it. Together, they would protect the Whispering Forest and ensure that its magic and wisdom would endure for generations to come.

# Chapter 8: The Tale of the Lost Prince

The Whispering Forest had whispered many secrets to Elara, Finn, Rowan, and Thistle, guiding them on their quest to protect its ancient magic. Yet, as they ventured deeper into the forest, they began to uncover a tale that had been buried for centuries—the story of a lost prince. This tale, shrouded in mystery and tragedy, hinted at a deeper connection to their quest and the challenges they faced.

It was a serene morning as they set out from their camp. The sun was just beginning to rise, casting a golden glow through the trees and illuminating the forest floor. The air was cool and crisp, filled with the scent of pine and blooming flowers. Vixen and Max trotted ahead, their senses alert for any signs of danger.

As they walked, Rowan began to share an old legend he had heard from the elder spirits of the forest. His deep voice carried a tone of reverence and solemnity, captivating his companions.

"Many centuries ago," Rowan began, "there was a young prince named Aldric, known for his bravery and kindness. He was the heir to a great kingdom that bordered the Whispering Forest. The people loved him, for he was wise beyond his years and had a heart full of compassion."

Elara and Finn listened intently, their curiosity piqued. They had heard many tales of the forest, but this one seemed to hold a special significance.

"Prince Aldric was also a skilled warrior and a devoted protector of the forest," Rowan continued. "He understood the importance of maintaining the balance between his kingdom and the magical realm of the forest. One day, he ventured into the Whispering Forest to seek the counsel of the guardian spirits. But he never returned."

Thistle's eyes widened with intrigue. "What happened to him?" she asked.

Rowan sighed, his expression somber. "No one knows for certain. Some say he was taken by dark forces that sought to corrupt the forest's magic. Others believe he was lost in the depths of the forest, unable to find his way back. His disappearance remains a mystery to this day."

Elara felt a deep sense of empathy for the lost prince. "If he was such a great protector of the forest, perhaps there is a way to find him," she said. "He could still be alive, waiting for someone to uncover the truth."

Finn nodded in agreement. "We should look for clues that might lead us to him," he said. "If Prince Aldric is still alive, he could be a valuable ally in our quest to protect the forest."

As they continued their journey, the whispers of the forest seemed to grow louder, guiding them toward a new path. The trees rustled softly, and the air was filled with a sense of anticipation. It was as if the forest itself wanted them to uncover the truth about the lost prince.

After several hours of walking, they reached a secluded glade. In the center of the glade stood a tall, ancient tree with bark that seemed to shimmer with an ethereal light. The tree exuded an aura of wisdom and strength, and its presence filled the glade with a sense of calm and tranquility.

"This tree is special," Elara said, her voice filled with awe. "I can feel its power. It must be connected to Prince Aldric's story."

Rowan nodded, his eyes scanning the tree for any signs of a hidden message. "The tree may hold clues that can help us find the prince," he said. "We need to look closely."

As they approached the tree, they noticed a series of intricate carvings etched into its bark. The carvings depicted scenes from Prince Aldric's life, from his early years as a young prince to his journey into the Whispering Forest. Each image was detailed and lifelike, telling the story of a brave and compassionate leader.

Finn traced his fingers over the carvings, feeling a sense of connection to the lost prince. "These carvings are like a record of his life," he said. "But there's something more here. Look at this."

He pointed to a section of the tree where the carvings seemed to form a pattern, creating a series of symbols and runes. The runes pulsed with a faint, blue light, as if holding a hidden message.

Elara examined the runes closely, her mind working to decipher their meaning. "The runes speak of a hidden path," she said. "A path that leads to the heart of the forest, where the prince may still be alive. We need to follow these clues and find the hidden path."

Thistle's eyes sparkled with excitement. "This could be the key to finding Prince Aldric," she said. "We should follow the runes and see where they lead."

Rowan nodded in agreement. "The forest is guiding us," he said. "We must trust in its wisdom and continue our journey."

With renewed determination, Elara, Finn, Rowan, and Thistle set out to follow the clues left by the runes. The whispers of the forest guided them, filling their minds with a sense of purpose and clarity. They knew that the journey ahead would be challenging, but they were ready to face whatever obstacles lay in their path.

As they ventured deeper into the forest, the runes led them to a series of hidden landmarks and ancient relics. Each clue brought them closer to uncovering the truth about Prince Aldric's fate. They navigated treacherous terrain, crossed rushing rivers, and faced cunning creatures that sought to impede their progress. But with each trial, their bond grew stronger, and their determination never wavered.

One particularly difficult challenge came in the form of a series of ancient stone pillars that blocked their path. The pillars were covered in intricate carvings and runes, creating a formidable barrier that seemed impossible to overcome.

"We need to decipher the runes to pass through the pillars," Elara said, her voice filled with determination. "The clues we've found so far must hold the key."

Finn examined the pillars closely, his mind working to decipher the runes. "The runes speak of balance and harmony, of light and dark," he said. "We need to find the right combination of symbols to unlock the pillars' magic."

Thistle's eyes sparkled with excitement. "I recognize some of these runes," she said. "They speak of the ancient magic of the forest, of the balance between light and dark. We need to trust in the wisdom of the forest and find the right combination."

Elara, Finn, Rowan, and Thistle worked together, carefully arranging the runes to create the right combination. As they placed the final symbol, the pillars began to glow with a soft, blue light. The ground beneath their feet seemed to hum with energy, and the pillars slowly began to part, creating a path that led deeper into the forest.

"We did it," Elara said, her voice filled with triumph. "The path is open. We need to continue following the clues."

As they walked along the newly revealed path, the whispers of the forest grew louder, filling their minds with a sense of calm and clarity. They knew that they were on the right track, and that the forest was guiding them toward the truth.

The path led them to a secluded cave, hidden deep within the heart of the forest. The entrance to the cave was covered in moss and vines, creating an almost impenetrable barrier. But the whispers of the forest urged them forward, and they knew that the cave held the key to uncovering the truth about Prince Aldric.

"This cave must be the final clue," Finn said, his voice filled with determination. "We need to find a way inside."

Rowan examined the entrance to the cave, his eyes scanning for any signs of a hidden passage. "There must be a way to open the entrance," he said. "The clues we've found so far must hold the key."

Thistle darted ahead, her nimble form easily navigating the tangled vines. "I think I see something," she called out, pointing to a series of runes carved into the rock.

Elara and Finn followed Thistle, carefully examining the runes. The runes pulsed with a faint, blue light, as if holding a hidden message.

"The runes speak of balance and harmony, of light and dark," Elara said thoughtfully. "We need to find the right words to activate the cave's magic."

Rowan nodded in agreement. "The cave is a guardian of the forest's wisdom," he said. "We need to speak the words of truth and purity to unlock its magic."

Elara and Finn joined hands, focusing their minds and hearts on the runes. They drew on the wisdom and strength of the forest, speaking the words that their hearts held.

"Ancient cave, guardian of the forest's wisdom," Elara began, her voice steady and clear. "We seek the guidance and protection of the forest. We have come with pure intent and open hearts. Show us the path that fate has sent."

As Elara spoke the words, the runes began to glow with a soft, blue light. The ground beneath their feet seemed to hum with energy, and the entrance to the cave slowly began to open, revealing a hidden passage that led deeper into the cave.

"We did it," Finn said, his voice filled with triumph. "The path is open. We need to continue following the clues."

As they ventured deeper into the cave, the air grew cooler and filled with an otherworldly energy. The walls of the cave were covered in intricate carvings and runes, telling the story of Prince Aldric's journey into the forest. Each image was detailed and lifelike, creating a vivid record of the prince's life.

At the end of the passage, they reached a small, hidden chamber. In the center of the chamber stood a tall, imposing figure draped in dark, flowing robes. His hair was long and black, and his eyes glowed with an otherworldly light. He exuded an aura of power and mystery, and his presence filled the chamber with a sense of tension and anticipation.

"Welcome, travelers," the figure said, his voice like the rustle of leaves in the wind. "I am Aldric, the lost prince of the Whispering Forest. I have been waiting for you."

Elara and Finn stepped forward, their hearts filled with a mixture of fear and determination. They had uncovered the truth about the lost prince, and they were ready to face whatever challenges lay ahead.

"We seek your guidance and protection," Elara said, her voice steady. "We are on a quest to protect the Whispering Forest and uncover its secrets. We need your help to continue our journey."

Aldric's eyes narrowed, and a faint smile played at the corners of his lips. "Many have come seeking my guidance and protection," he said. "But few have proven themselves worthy. You must face my trials and earn my respect before I will grant you my aid."

Finn stepped forward, his eyes blazing with determination. "We are ready to face your trials," he said. "We will do whatever it takes to protect the forest."

Aldric's smile widened, and he raised his hands, casting a series of intricate spells. The air around them shimmered with magic, and the chamber was transformed into a labyrinth of twisting paths and hidden dangers.

"Your first trial is a test of courage and resolve," Aldric said. "You must navigate this labyrinth and reach the heart of the chamber. Only then will you prove yourselves worthy of my guidance."

Elara, Finn, Rowan, and Thistle nodded, their hearts filled with determination. They knew that the labyrinth would be filled with challenges, but they were ready to face whatever obstacles lay ahead.

As they entered the labyrinth, the paths twisted and turned, creating a disorienting maze of rock and shadows. The air was thick with an otherworldly energy, and the whispers of the forest seemed to fade into the background.

"We need to stay together and trust in each other," Elara said, her voice steady. "The labyrinth is designed to test our courage and resolve. We must not lose our way."

Rowan nodded, his eyes scanning the paths for any sign of danger. "We need to keep moving and stay focused," he said. "The labyrinth is filled with traps and illusions. We must be vigilant."

Thistle darted ahead, her nimble form easily navigating the twisting paths. "I can sense the magic of the labyrinth," she said. "We need to follow the path of light. It will lead us to the heart of the chamber."

Elara and Finn followed Thistle, carefully making their way through the labyrinth. The paths were filled with hidden traps and illusions, designed to confuse and deceive them. They encountered shadowy figures that sought to block their way, but they stood their ground and pressed on, determined to reach the heart of the chamber.

As they ventured deeper into the labyrinth, they felt a growing sense of tension and anticipation. The paths grew darker and more twisted, and the air was filled with an eerie silence. They knew that they were nearing the heart of the chamber, and that the most difficult part of the trial lay ahead.

After what felt like hours of navigating the labyrinth, they reached a small clearing. In the center of the clearing stood a tall, ancient tree with dark, shadowy leaves that seemed to absorb the light. The tree swayed gently, its branches forming a natural canopy that cast dappled shadows on the ground.

"This must be the heart of the chamber," Finn said, his voice filled with awe. "We need to prove our worthiness to Aldric."

As they approached the tree, they felt a deep, resonant energy emanating from its trunk and branches. The whispers of the forest grew louder, filling their minds with a sense of calm and clarity. They knew that they were in the right place, and that the tree held the key to the next step of their journey.

Aldric appeared before them, his eyes glowing with an otherworldly light. "You have reached the heart of the chamber," he said. "But your trials are not yet over. You must face one final test to prove your worthiness."

He raised his hands, casting a powerful spell that enveloped the clearing in a shimmering light. The ground beneath their feet seemed to hum with energy, and a series of ancient runes appeared on the trunk of the tree.

"This is a test of wisdom and insight," Aldric said. "You must decipher the runes and unlock the magic of the tree. Only then will you earn my respect and receive the artifact you seek."

Elara, Finn, Rowan, and Thistle examined the runes, their minds working to decipher their meaning. The runes were written in an ancient language, and they knew that they held the key to unlocking the tree's magic.

"The runes speak of balance and harmony, of light and dark," Elara said thoughtfully. "We need to find the right words to activate the tree's magic."

Rowan nodded, his eyes scanning the runes for any clues. "The tree is a guardian of the forest's wisdom," he said. "We need to speak the words of truth and purity to unlock its magic."

Thistle's eyes sparkled with excitement. "I recognize some of these runes," she said. "They speak of the ancient magic of the forest, of the balance between light and dark. We need to trust in the wisdom of the forest and speak the words that our hearts hold."

Elara and Finn joined hands, focusing their minds and hearts on the runes. They drew on the wisdom and strength of the forest, speaking the words that their hearts held.

"Ancient tree, guardian of the chamber's wisdom," Elara began, her voice steady and clear. "We seek the guidance and protection of the forest. We have come with pure intent and open hearts. Show us the path that fate has sent."

As Elara spoke the words, the runes began to glow with a soft, blue light. The ground beneath their feet seemed to hum with energy, and the tree's branches swayed gently, as if acknowledging their words.

"You have spoken the words of truth and purity," Aldric said, his voice filled with approval. "You have proven yourselves worthy of my respect. I will grant you the artifact you seek."

He raised his hands, casting a spell that caused the tree to shimmer and glow with an ethereal light. A small, intricately carved wooden box appeared at the base of the tree, its surface covered in ancient runes.

"This box contains a magical artifact that will aid you on your quest," Aldric said. "It holds the essence of the chamber's magic, a powerful tool that will help you protect the forest and stand against the darkness. Use it wisely and with respect."

Elara and Finn stepped forward, their hearts filled with gratitude and determination. They carefully picked up the wooden box, feeling its smooth surface and the warmth of its magic.

"Thank you, Aldric," Elara said, her voice filled with gratitude. "We will use the artifact to protect the forest and continue our quest."

Aldric smiled, his eyes twinkling with approval. "You have earned my respect and my guidance," he said. "The path to the deeper part of the forest lies before you. Follow the whispers and trust in the wisdom of the forest. You are ready to face whatever challenges lie ahead."

With renewed hope and strength, Elara, Finn, Rowan, and Thistle set out on the next leg of their journey, guided by the whispers and the wisdom of the forest. They knew that the path ahead would be fraught with danger and deception, but they were ready to face whatever obstacles lay in their path.

As they ventured deeper into the forest, they encountered a series of trials and challenges that tested their courage, intelligence, and bond with the land. They navigated treacherous terrain, crossed rushing rivers, and faced cunning creatures that sought to impede their progress. But with each trial, their bond grew stronger, and their determination never wavered.

Their adventure was far from over, but they faced it with courage and determination. The encounter with Aldric, the lost prince, had given them new allies and powerful tools, and they were stronger for it. Together, they would protect the Whispering Forest and ensure that its magic and wisdom would endure for generations to come.

# Chapter 9: The Guardian of the Bridge

As Elara, Finn, Rowan, and Thistle continued their journey through the Whispering Forest, they grew ever closer to the heart of the forest, where the ancient magic and ultimate answers awaited. Their path was guided by the whispers of the forest, and they knew that many more challenges lay ahead. One such challenge was the Guardian of the Bridge, a formidable creature that tested the courage and determination of all who sought to cross into the deepest parts of the forest.

The air was crisp and cool as they set out from their camp that morning. The sun filtered through the dense canopy of trees, casting dappled shadows on the forest floor. Vixen and Max trotted ahead, their senses alert for any signs of danger. The group walked in silence, each of them lost in their thoughts about the trials they had already faced and the ones that still awaited them.

After several hours of walking, the whispers of the forest guided them to a narrow path that wound through a dense thicket of trees. The path was overgrown with vines and brambles, creating a natural barrier that seemed almost impenetrable.

"This must be the way to the bridge," Rowan said, his deep voice cutting through the silence. "We need to find a way through."

Thistle darted ahead, her nimble form easily navigating the tangled vines. "I think I see something," she called out, pointing to a faint glow emanating from the base of one of the trees.

Elara and Finn followed Thistle, carefully making their way through the tangled undergrowth. As they reached the source of the glow, they found a small, intricately carved stone set into the ground. The stone was covered in ancient runes that pulsed with a soft, blue light.

"This stone must be the key to opening the path," Elara said, her voice filled with wonder. "We need to decipher the runes and unlock its magic."

Finn examined the runes closely, his mind working to decipher their meaning. "The runes speak of balance and harmony, of light and dark," he said. "We need to find the right words to activate the stone's magic."

Rowan nodded in agreement. "The path is a guardian of the forest's wisdom," he said. "We need to speak the words of truth and purity to unlock its magic."

Elara, Finn, Rowan, and Thistle joined hands, focusing their minds and hearts on the runes. They drew on the wisdom and strength of the forest, speaking the words that their hearts held.

"Ancient path, guardian of the forest's wisdom," Elara began, her voice steady and clear. "We seek the guidance and protection of the forest. We have come with pure intent and open hearts. Show us the way."

As Elara spoke the words, the runes began to glow more brightly, and the ground beneath their feet seemed to hum with energy. The vines and brambles slowly began to part, creating a narrow passage that led deeper into the forest.

"We did it," Finn said, his voice filled with triumph. "The path is open. We need to continue following the whispers."

As they ventured deeper into the forest, the air grew cooler and filled with an otherworldly energy. The trees around them seemed to grow taller and more imposing, their branches forming a dense canopy that blocked out much of the sunlight. The whispers of the forest guided them, filling their minds with a sense of purpose and clarity.

After several hours of walking, they reached a wide, rushing river. The river was deep and fast-flowing, its waters churning with an almost unnatural energy. A narrow, ancient bridge spanned the river, its weathered stones covered in moss and ivy. At the far end of the bridge stood a giant creature, its massive form blocking the way.

The Guardian of the Bridge was a formidable sight. Standing over ten feet tall, the creature had the body of a bear, covered in thick, dark fur, and the head of an eagle, with piercing golden eyes and a sharp, hooked beak. Its massive paws ended in razor-sharp claws, and its wings were folded against its back. The creature exuded an aura of power and strength, and its presence filled the air with a sense of tension and anticipation.

"Welcome, travelers," the Guardian of the Bridge said, its voice deep and resonant, like the rumble of distant thunder. "I am the Guardian of the Bridge, and I have been expecting you."

Elara and Finn stepped forward, their hearts filled with a mixture of fear and determination. They knew that this confrontation would be one of the most challenging yet, but they were ready to face it together.

"We seek passage across the bridge," Elara said, her voice steady. "We are on a quest to protect the Whispering Forest and uncover its secrets. We need to cross the bridge to continue our journey."

The Guardian's golden eyes narrowed, and a faint smile played at the corners of its beak. "Many have come seeking passage across this bridge," it said. "But few have proven themselves worthy. You must face my trials and earn the right to cross."

Finn stepped forward, his eyes blazing with determination. "We are ready to face your trials," he said. "We will do whatever it takes to protect the forest."

The Guardian's smile widened, and it raised one massive paw, casting a series of intricate spells. The air around them shimmered with magic, and the bridge was transformed into a labyrinth of twisting paths and hidden dangers.

"Your first trial is a test of courage and resolve," the Guardian said. "You must navigate this labyrinth and reach the heart of the bridge. Only then will you prove yourselves worthy of passage."

Elara, Finn, Rowan, and Thistle nodded, their hearts filled with determination. They knew that the labyrinth would be filled with challenges, but they were ready to face whatever obstacles lay ahead.

As they entered the labyrinth, the paths twisted and turned, creating a disorienting maze of stone and shadows. The air was thick with an otherworldly energy, and the whispers of the forest seemed to fade into the background.

"We need to stay together and trust in each other," Elara said, her voice steady. "The labyrinth is designed to test our courage and resolve. We must not lose our way."

Rowan nodded, his eyes scanning the paths for any sign of danger. "We need to keep moving and stay focused," he said. "The labyrinth is filled with traps and illusions. We must be vigilant."

Thistle darted ahead, her nimble form easily navigating the twisting paths. "I can sense the magic of the labyrinth," she said. "We need to follow the path of light. It will lead us to the heart of the bridge."

Elara and Finn followed Thistle, carefully making their way through the labyrinth. The paths were filled with hidden traps and illusions, designed to confuse and deceive them. They encountered shadowy figures that sought to block their way, but they stood their ground and pressed on, determined to reach the heart of the bridge.

As they ventured deeper into the labyrinth, they felt a growing sense of tension and anticipation. The paths grew darker and more twisted, and the air was filled with an eerie silence. They knew that they were nearing the heart of the bridge, and that the most difficult part of the trial lay ahead.

After what felt like hours of navigating the labyrinth, they reached a small clearing. In the center of the clearing stood a tall, ancient tree with dark, shadowy leaves that seemed to absorb the light. The tree swayed gently, its branches forming a natural canopy that cast dappled shadows on the ground.

"This must be the heart of the bridge," Finn said, his voice filled with awe. "We need to prove our worthiness to the Guardian."

As they approached the tree, they felt a deep, resonant energy emanating from its trunk and branches. The whispers of the forest grew louder, filling their minds with a sense of calm and clarity. They knew that they were in the right place, and that the tree held the key to the next step of their journey.

The Guardian of the Bridge appeared before them, its golden eyes glowing with an otherworldly light. "You have reached the heart of the bridge," it said. "But your trials are not yet over. You must face one final test to prove your worthiness."

It raised its massive paw, casting a powerful spell that enveloped the clearing in a shimmering light. The ground beneath their feet seemed to hum with energy, and a series of ancient runes appeared on the trunk of the tree.

"This is a test of wisdom and insight," the Guardian said. "You must decipher the runes and unlock the magic of the tree. Only then will you earn the right to cross the bridge."

Elara, Finn, Rowan, and Thistle examined the runes, their minds working to decipher their meaning. The runes were written in an ancient language, and they knew that they held the key to unlocking the tree's magic.

"The runes speak of balance and harmony, of light and dark," Elara said thoughtfully. "We need to find the right words to activate the tree's magic."

Rowan nodded, his eyes scanning the runes for any clues. "The tree is a guardian of the forest's wisdom," he said. "We need to speak the words of truth and purity to unlock its magic."

Thistle's eyes sparkled with excitement. "I recognize some of these runes," she said. "They speak of the ancient magic of the forest, of the balance between light and dark. We need to trust in the wisdom of the forest and speak the words that our hearts hold."

Elara and Finn joined hands, focusing their minds and hearts on the runes. They drew on the wisdom and strength of the forest, speaking the words that their hearts held.

"Ancient tree, guardian of the bridge's wisdom," Elara began, her voice steady and clear. "We seek the guidance and protection of the forest. We have come with pure intent and open hearts. Show us the path that fate has sent."

As Elara spoke the words, the runes began to glow with a soft, blue light. The ground beneath their feet seemed to hum with energy, and the tree's branches swayed gently, as if acknowledging their words.

"You have spoken the words of truth and purity," the Guardian said, its voice filled with approval. "You have proven yourselves worthy of crossing the bridge. I will grant you passage."

The Guardian raised its massive paw once more, casting a spell that caused the tree to shimmer and glow with an ethereal light. A small, intricately carved wooden box appeared at the base of the tree, its surface covered in ancient runes.

"This box contains a magical artifact that will aid you on your quest," the Guardian said. "It holds the essence of the bridge's magic, a powerful tool that will help you protect the forest and stand against the darkness. Use it wisely and with respect."

Elara and Finn stepped forward, their hearts filled with gratitude and determination. They carefully picked up the wooden box, feeling its smooth surface and the warmth of its magic.

"Thank you, Guardian," Elara said, her voice filled with gratitude. "We will use the artifact to protect the forest and continue our quest."

The Guardian smiled, its golden eyes twinkling with approval. "You have earned my respect and my guidance," it said. "The path to the heart of the forest lies before you. Follow the whispers and trust in the wisdom of the forest. You are ready to face whatever challenges lie ahead."

With renewed hope and strength, Elara, Finn, Rowan, and Thistle set out to cross the bridge, guided by the whispers and the wisdom of the forest. They knew that the path ahead would be fraught with danger and deception, but they were ready to face whatever obstacles lay in their path.

As they ventured across the bridge, the air grew cooler and filled with an otherworldly energy. The bridge's ancient stones were covered in moss and ivy, creating a sense of timelessness and mystery. The river below rushed with a powerful current, its waters churning with an almost unnatural energy.

Halfway across the bridge, the whispers of the forest grew louder, filling their minds with a sense of calm and clarity. They knew that they were on the right path, and that the forest was guiding them toward their ultimate goal.

After several minutes of walking, they reached the far side of the bridge. The path before them led deeper into the heart of the forest, where the ancient magic and ultimate answers awaited. They knew that their journey was far from over, but with the wisdom and strength they had gained, they felt ready to face whatever challenges lay ahead.

The forest around them grew denser and more imposing, its ancient trees casting long shadows on the forest floor. The air was thick with the scent of pine and blooming flowers, and the whispers of the forest filled their minds with a sense of purpose and determination.

As they continued their journey, they encountered a series of trials and challenges that tested their courage, intelligence, and bond with the land. They navigated treacherous terrain, crossed rushing rivers, and faced cunning creatures that sought to impede their progress. But with each trial, their bond grew stronger, and their determination never wavered.

One particularly difficult challenge came in the form of a dense, shadowy thicket that seemed to block their path. The thicket was filled with twisted vines and thorny bushes, creating a nearly impenetrable barrier. The whispers of the forest urged them to find a way through, but the path seemed impossible.

"We need to find a way around this thicket," Finn said, his voice filled with determination. "The heart of the forest must be on the other side."

Rowan examined the thicket, his eyes scanning for any sign of a hidden path. "There must be a way through," he said. "We just need to find it."

Thistle darted ahead, her nimble form easily navigating the tangled vines. "I think I see something," she called out, pointing to a narrow gap in the thicket.

Elara and Finn followed Thistle, carefully making their way through the narrow gap. The vines scratched at their skin and clothing, but they pressed on, determined to reach the other side. Vixen and Max stayed close, their senses alert for any signs of danger.

After what felt like hours of struggling through the thicket, they finally emerged into a small clearing. The clearing was bathed in the soft glow of the moonlight, and in the center stood a tall, ancient tree with dark, shadowy leaves that seemed to absorb the light. The tree swayed gently, its branches forming a natural canopy that cast dappled shadows on the ground.

"This must be the heart of the forest," Finn said, his voice filled with awe. "We need to prove our worthiness to the Guardian."

As they approached the tree, they felt a deep, resonant energy emanating from its trunk and branches. The whispers of the forest grew louder, filling their minds with a sense of calm and clarity. They knew that they were in the right place, and that the tree held the key to the next step of their journey.

The Guardian of the Bridge appeared before them, its golden eyes glowing with an otherworldly light. "You have reached the heart of the forest," it said. "But your trials are not yet over. You must face one final test to prove your worthiness."

It raised its massive paw, casting a powerful spell that enveloped the clearing in a shimmering light. The ground beneath their feet seemed to hum with energy, and a series of ancient runes appeared on the trunk of the tree.

"This is a test of wisdom and insight," the Guardian said. "You must decipher the runes and unlock the magic of the tree. Only then will you earn the right to cross into the heart of the forest."

Elara, Finn, Rowan, and Thistle examined the runes, their minds working to decipher their meaning. The runes were written in an ancient language, and they knew that they held the key to unlocking the tree's magic.

"The runes speak of balance and harmony, of light and dark," Elara said thoughtfully. "We need to find the right words to activate the tree's magic."

Rowan nodded, his eyes scanning the runes for any clues. "The tree is a guardian of the forest's wisdom," he said. "We need to speak the words of truth and purity to unlock its magic."

Thistle's eyes sparkled with excitement. "I recognize some of these runes," she said. "They speak of the ancient magic of the forest, of the balance between light and dark. We need to trust in the wisdom of the forest and speak the words that our hearts hold."

Elara and Finn joined hands, focusing their minds and hearts on the runes. They drew on the wisdom and strength of the forest, speaking the words that their hearts held.

"Ancient tree, guardian of the forest's heart," Elara began, her voice steady and clear. "We seek the guidance and protection of the forest. We have come with pure intent and open hearts. Show us the path that fate has sent."

As Elara spoke the words, the runes began to glow with a soft, blue light. The ground beneath their feet seemed to hum with energy, and the tree's branches swayed gently, as if acknowledging their words.

"You have spoken the words of truth and purity," the Guardian said, its voice filled with approval. "You have proven yourselves worthy of crossing into the heart of the forest. I will grant you passage."

The Guardian raised its massive paw once more, casting a spell that caused the tree to shimmer and glow with an ethereal light. A small, intricately carved wooden box appeared at the base of the tree, its surface covered in ancient runes.

"This box contains a magical artifact that will aid you on your quest," the Guardian said. "It holds the essence of the forest's heart, a powerful tool that will help you protect the forest and stand against the darkness. Use it wisely and with respect."

Elara and Finn stepped forward, their hearts filled with gratitude and determination. They carefully picked up the wooden box, feeling its smooth surface and the warmth of its magic.

"Thank you, Guardian," Elara said, her voice filled with gratitude. "We will use the artifact to protect the forest and continue our quest."

The Guardian smiled, its golden eyes twinkling with approval. "You have earned my respect and my guidance," it said. "The path to the heart of the forest lies before you. Follow the whispers and trust in the wisdom of the forest. You are ready to face whatever challenges lie ahead."

With renewed hope and strength, Elara, Finn, Rowan, and Thistle set out on the next leg of their journey, guided by the whispers and the wisdom of the forest. They knew that the path ahead would be fraught with danger and deception, but they were ready to face whatever obstacles lay in their path.

As they ventured deeper into the forest, they encountered a series of trials and challenges that tested their courage, intelligence, and bond with the land. They navigated treacherous terrain, crossed rushing rivers, and faced cunning creatures that sought to impede their progress. But with each trial, their bond grew stronger, and their determination never wavered.

Their adventure was far from over, but they faced it with courage and determination. The encounter with the Guardian of the Bridge had given them new allies and powerful tools, and they were stronger for it. Together, they would protect the Whispering Forest and ensure that its magic and wisdom would endure for generations to come.

# Chapter 10: The Cave of Whispers

The journey through the Whispering Forest had been a series of trials, each more challenging than the last. Elara, Finn, Rowan, and Thistle had proven their worthiness time and again, guided by the forest's whispers and their unwavering determination. As they ventured deeper into the heart of the forest, they knew their next destination was the Cave of Whispers, a place where the ancient spirits of the forest resided. It was here that they hoped to uncover hidden truths about the forest's history and receive guidance on their quest for the Silver Leaf.

The air was cool and crisp as they set out that morning. The sun had just begun to rise, casting a golden glow through the dense canopy of trees. The forest was alive with the sounds of birds singing and leaves rustling in the gentle breeze. Vixen and Max trotted ahead, their senses alert for any signs of danger.

As they walked, Rowan shared what he knew about the Cave of Whispers. His deep voice carried a tone of reverence and solemnity, captivating his companions.

"The Cave of Whispers is a sacred place," Rowan began. "It is said to be the dwelling of the forest's ancient spirits, guardians of its magic and wisdom. The cave is a place of great power, where the voices of the past can be heard, and hidden truths can be uncovered."

Elara and Finn listened intently, their curiosity piqued. They had heard many tales of the forest, but this one seemed to hold a special significance.

"The spirits within the cave are ancient and wise," Rowan continued. "They have witnessed the history of the forest, from its creation to the present day. They hold the knowledge of the forest's magic and the secrets of its past."

Thistle's eyes sparkled with excitement. "If we can listen to the voices of the past and uncover these hidden truths, it could help us on our quest," she said. "We need to find the Cave of Whispers and seek the guidance of the spirits."

Elara felt a deep sense of purpose. "The spirits may hold the key to finding the Silver Leaf," she said. "We need to uncover the truth and continue our journey."

As they continued their journey, the whispers of the forest grew louder, guiding them toward a narrow path that wound through a dense thicket of trees. The path was overgrown with vines and brambles, creating a natural barrier that seemed almost impenetrable.

"This must be the way to the cave," Rowan said, his deep voice cutting through the silence. "We need to find a way through."

Thistle darted ahead, her nimble form easily navigating the tangled vines. "I think I see something," she called out, pointing to a faint glow emanating from the base of one of the trees.

Elara and Finn followed Thistle, carefully making their way through the tangled undergrowth. As they reached the source of the glow, they found a small, intricately carved stone set into the ground. The stone was covered in ancient runes that pulsed with a soft, blue light.

"This stone must be the key to opening the path," Elara said, her voice filled with wonder. "We need to decipher the runes and unlock its magic."

Finn examined the runes closely, his mind working to decipher their meaning. "The runes speak of balance and harmony, of light and dark," he said. "We need to find the right words to activate the stone's magic."

Rowan nodded in agreement. "The path is a guardian of the forest's wisdom," he said. "We need to speak the words of truth and purity to unlock its magic."

Elara, Finn, Rowan, and Thistle joined hands, focusing their minds and hearts on the runes. They drew on the wisdom and strength of the forest, speaking the words that their hearts held.

"Ancient path, guardian of the forest's wisdom," Elara began, her voice steady and clear. "We seek the guidance and protection of the forest. We have come with pure intent and open hearts. Show us the way."

As Elara spoke the words, the runes began to glow more brightly, and the ground beneath their feet seemed to hum with energy. The vines and brambles slowly began to part, creating a narrow passage that led deeper into the forest.

"We did it," Finn said, his voice filled with triumph. "The path is open. We need to continue following the whispers."

As they ventured deeper into the forest, the air grew cooler and filled with an otherworldly energy. The trees around them seemed to grow taller and more imposing, their branches forming a dense canopy that blocked out much of the sunlight. The whispers of the forest guided them, filling their minds with a sense of purpose and clarity.

After several hours of walking, they reached a secluded glade. In the center of the glade stood a tall, ancient tree with bark that seemed to shimmer with an ethereal light. The tree exuded an aura of wisdom and strength, and its presence filled the glade with a sense of calm and tranquility.

"This tree is special," Elara said, her voice filled with awe. "I can feel its power. It must be connected to the Cave of Whispers."

Rowan nodded, his eyes scanning the tree for any signs of a hidden message. "The tree may hold clues that can help us find the cave," he said. "We need to look closely."

As they approached the tree, they noticed a series of intricate carvings etched into its bark. The carvings depicted scenes from the forest's history, from its creation to the present day. Each image was detailed and lifelike, telling the story of the forest's magic and the guardian spirits that protected it.

Finn traced his fingers over the carvings, feeling a sense of connection to the forest. "These carvings are like a record of the forest's history," he said. "But there's something more here. Look at this."

He pointed to a section of the tree where the carvings seemed to form a pattern, creating a series of symbols and runes. The runes pulsed with a faint, blue light, as if holding a hidden message.

Elara examined the runes closely, her mind working to decipher their meaning. "The runes speak of a hidden path," she said. "A path that leads to the Cave of Whispers. We need to follow these clues and find the hidden path."

Thistle's eyes sparkled with excitement. "This could be the key to finding the cave," she said. "We should follow the runes and see where they lead."

Rowan nodded in agreement. "The forest is guiding us," he said. "We must trust in its wisdom and continue our journey."

With renewed determination, Elara, Finn, Rowan, and Thistle set out to follow the clues left by the runes. The whispers of the forest guided them, filling their minds with a sense of purpose and clarity. They knew that the journey ahead would be challenging, but they were ready to face whatever obstacles lay in their path.

As they ventured deeper into the forest, the runes led them to a series of hidden landmarks and ancient relics. Each clue brought them closer to uncovering the truth about the Cave of Whispers. They navigated treacherous terrain, crossed rushing rivers, and faced cunning creatures that sought to impede their progress. But with each trial, their bond grew stronger, and their determination never wavered.

One particularly difficult challenge came in the form of a dense, shadowy thicket that seemed to block their path. The thicket was filled with twisted vines and thorny bushes, creating a nearly impenetrable barrier. The whispers of the forest urged them to find a way through, but the path seemed impossible.

"We need to find a way around this thicket," Finn said, his voice filled with determination. "The cave must be on the other side."

Rowan examined the thicket, his eyes scanning for any sign of a hidden path. "There must be a way through," he said. "We just need to find it."

Thistle darted ahead, her nimble form easily navigating the tangled vines. "I think I see something," she called out, pointing to a narrow gap in the thicket.

Elara and Finn followed Thistle, carefully making their way through the narrow gap. The vines scratched at their skin and clothing, but they pressed on, determined to reach the other side. Vixen and Max stayed close, their senses alert for any signs of danger.

After what felt like hours of struggling through the thicket, they finally emerged into a small clearing. The clearing was bathed in the soft glow of the moonlight, and in the center stood a tall, ancient tree with dark, shadowy leaves that seemed to absorb the light. The tree swayed gently, its branches forming a natural canopy that cast dappled shadows on the ground.

"This must be the entrance to the cave," Finn said, his voice filled with awe. "We need to prove our worthiness to the spirits."

As they approached the tree, they felt a deep, resonant energy emanating from its trunk and branches. The whispers of the forest grew louder, filling their minds with a sense of calm and clarity. They knew that they were in the right place, and that the tree held the key to the next step of their journey.

The ancient tree began to glow with an ethereal light, and a hidden passageway opened at its base, revealing a dark tunnel that led deep underground.

"This is it," Rowan said, his voice filled with determination. "The Cave of Whispers lies ahead. We need to enter and seek the guidance of the spirits."

Elara, Finn, Rowan, and Thistle stepped forward, their hearts filled with resolve. They knew that the cave would be filled with challenges, but they were ready to face whatever obstacles lay ahead.

As they entered the tunnel, the air grew cooler and filled with an otherworldly energy. The walls of the tunnel were covered in intricate carvings and runes, telling the story of the forest's history and the guardian spirits that protected it. The whispers of the forest grew louder, echoing through the tunnel and filling their minds with a sense of purpose and clarity.

After several minutes of walking, they emerged into a vast, cavernous chamber. The chamber was filled with a soft, blue light that seemed to emanate from the walls themselves. The air was thick with the presence of ancient magic, and the whispers of the forest echoed all around them.

"This is the Cave of Whispers," Elara said, her voice filled with awe. "We need to listen to the voices of the past and uncover the hidden truths."

As they ventured deeper into the cave, the whispers grew louder and more distinct. The voices of the ancient spirits seemed to call out to them, guiding them toward the heart of the cave.

In the center of the chamber stood a tall, ancient stone altar, covered in intricate carvings and runes. The altar pulsed with a soft, blue light, and the air around it seemed to hum with energy.

"This altar must hold the key to uncovering the hidden truths," Rowan said, his voice filled with reverence. "We need to listen to the voices and seek their guidance."

Elara, Finn, Rowan, and Thistle approached the altar, their hearts filled with anticipation. They closed their eyes and focused their minds, listening to the whispers of the ancient spirits.

The voices grew clearer, filling their minds with a sense of calm and clarity. The spirits spoke of the forest's history, from its creation to the present day. They told of the guardian spirits that protected the forest, and the dark forces that sought to corrupt its magic.

"The forest was created by the guardian spirits," one voice said. "They wove their magic into the very fabric of the land, creating a place of beauty and wonder."

"But darkness has always sought to consume the forest," another voice added. "Evil forces have tried to corrupt its magic and destroy its balance."

Elara and Finn listened intently, their hearts filled with a sense of purpose. They knew that the spirits held the key to uncovering the truth and finding the Silver Leaf.

"The Silver Leaf is a powerful artifact," a third voice said. "It holds the essence of the forest's magic and the wisdom of the guardian spirits. It is hidden deep within the heart of the forest, protected by powerful enchantments."

"But the path to the Silver Leaf is fraught with danger," the first voice warned. "Only those who prove themselves worthy can unlock its magic and use it to protect the forest."

As the voices continued to speak, a vision began to form in Elara's mind. She saw a hidden glade, bathed in the soft glow of moonlight. In the center of the glade stood a tall, ancient tree with silver leaves that shimmered in the breeze. The tree exuded an aura of wisdom and strength, and its presence filled the glade with a sense of calm and tranquility.

"This is the tree that holds the Silver Leaf," the third voice said. "You must find this glade and unlock the magic of the tree. Only then will you be able to use the Silver Leaf to protect the forest."

Elara opened her eyes, her heart filled with determination. "I saw a vision," she said. "A hidden glade with a tree that holds the Silver Leaf. We need to find this glade and unlock the magic of the tree."

Finn nodded, his eyes filled with resolve. "The spirits have shown us the way," he said. "We need to follow the vision and continue our quest."

Rowan and Thistle nodded in agreement, their hearts filled with a sense of purpose. "The forest is guiding us," Rowan said. "We must trust in its wisdom and continue our journey."

With renewed determination, Elara, Finn, Rowan, and Thistle set out to follow the vision and find the hidden glade. The whispers of the forest guided them, filling their minds with a sense of purpose and clarity. They knew that the journey ahead would be challenging, but they were ready to face whatever obstacles lay in their path.

As they ventured deeper into the forest, the air grew cooler and filled with an otherworldly energy. The trees around them seemed to grow taller and more imposing, their branches forming a dense canopy that blocked out much of the sunlight. The whispers of the forest guided them, filling their minds with a sense of purpose and clarity.

After several hours of walking, they reached a secluded glade. In the center of the glade stood a tall, ancient tree with silver leaves that shimmered in the breeze. The tree exuded an aura of wisdom and strength, and its presence filled the glade with a sense of calm and tranquility.

"This is the glade from the vision," Elara said, her voice filled with awe. "The tree that holds the Silver Leaf."

As they approached the tree, they felt a deep, resonant energy emanating from its trunk and branches. The whispers of the forest grew louder, filling their minds with a sense of calm and clarity. They knew that they were in the right place, and that the tree held the key to unlocking the magic of the Silver Leaf.

"The runes on the tree must hold the key to unlocking its magic," Rowan said, his voice filled with determination. "We need to decipher the runes and speak the words that will unlock the magic of the tree."

Elara, Finn, Rowan, and Thistle examined the runes, their minds working to decipher their meaning. The runes were written in an ancient language, and they knew that they held the key to unlocking the tree's magic.

"The runes speak of balance and harmony, of light and dark," Elara said thoughtfully. "We need to find the right words to activate the tree's magic."

Rowan nodded, his eyes scanning the runes for any clues. "The tree is a guardian of the forest's wisdom," he said. "We need to speak the words of truth and purity to unlock its magic."

Thistle's eyes sparkled with excitement. "I recognize some of these runes," she said. "They speak of the ancient magic of the forest, of the balance between light and dark. We need to trust in the wisdom of the forest and speak the words that our hearts hold."

Elara and Finn joined hands, focusing their minds and hearts on the runes. They drew on the wisdom and strength of the forest, speaking the words that their hearts held.

"Ancient tree, guardian of the Silver Leaf's magic," Elara began, her voice steady and clear. "We seek the guidance and protection of the forest. We have come with pure intent and open hearts. Show us the way."

As Elara spoke the words, the runes began to glow with a soft, blue light. The ground beneath their feet seemed to hum with energy, and the tree's branches swayed gently, as if acknowledging their words.

"You have spoken the words of truth and purity," a deep, resonant voice said. "You have proven yourselves worthy of the Silver Leaf's magic. I will grant you its power."

The tree's silver leaves began to shimmer and glow with an ethereal light. A small, intricately carved wooden box appeared at the base of the tree, its surface covered in ancient runes.

"This box contains the Silver Leaf," the voice said. "It holds the essence of the forest's magic and the wisdom of the guardian spirits. Use it wisely and with respect."

Elara and Finn stepped forward, their hearts filled with gratitude and determination. They carefully picked up the wooden box, feeling its smooth surface and the warmth of its magic.

"Thank you, guardian," Elara said, her voice filled with gratitude. "We will use the Silver Leaf to protect the forest and continue our quest."

The voice smiled, its presence filling the glade with a sense of approval. "You have earned my respect and my guidance," it said. "The path to the heart of the forest lies before you. Follow the whispers and trust in the wisdom of the forest. You are ready to face whatever challenges lie ahead."

With renewed hope and strength, Elara, Finn, Rowan, and Thistle set out on the next leg of their journey, guided by the whispers and the wisdom of the forest. They knew that the path ahead would be fraught with danger and deception, but they were ready to face whatever obstacles lay in their path.

As they ventured deeper into the forest, they encountered a series of trials and challenges that tested their courage, intelligence, and bond with the land. They navigated treacherous terrain, crossed rushing rivers, and faced cunning creatures that sought to impede their progress. But with each trial, their bond grew stronger, and their determination never wavered.

Their adventure was far from over, but they faced it with courage and determination. The encounter with the Cave of Whispers had given them new allies and powerful tools, and they were stronger for it. Together, they would protect the Whispering Forest and ensure that its magic and wisdom would endure for generations to come.

# Chapter 11: The Battle of Shadows

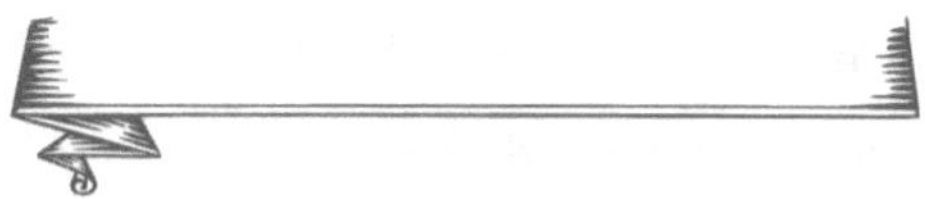

The Whispering Forest had guided Elara, Finn, Rowan, and Thistle through countless challenges and trials, but their greatest test was yet to come. As they ventured deeper into the heart of the forest, the whispers grew darker and more urgent, warning of an impending threat. A powerful dark force sought to consume the forest's magic and plunge it into eternal darkness. The time had come for them to confront this malevolent presence and protect the Whispering Forest.

The air was thick with tension as they set out that morning. The sun was hidden behind a blanket of dark clouds, casting an eerie shadow over the forest. The trees seemed to whisper warnings, their leaves rustling anxiously in the wind. Vixen and Max stayed close to Elara and Finn, their senses alert for any signs of danger.

As they walked, Rowan spoke of the dark force they were about to face. His deep voice was filled with a sense of urgency and determination.

"The darkness that threatens the forest is unlike any we have encountered before," Rowan said. "It is a powerful and ancient force, bent on consuming the forest's magic and corrupting its balance. We must be prepared for a fierce battle."

Elara and Finn listened intently, their hearts filled with a mixture of fear and resolve. They knew that this confrontation would be their most difficult challenge yet, but they were ready to face it together.

"The forest has guided us this far," Elara said, her voice steady. "We must trust in its wisdom and our own strength. We can protect the forest and stand against the darkness."

Thistle's eyes sparkled with determination. "We have faced many trials and grown stronger with each one," she said. "We are ready for this battle. We will protect the Whispering Forest."

As they continued their journey, the whispers of the forest grew louder, urging them forward. The path led them to a wide, open clearing, where the air was thick with an oppressive energy. In the center of the clearing stood a towering figure shrouded in darkness. Its eyes glowed with an eerie light, and its presence exuded a malevolent power.

"This is the source of the dark force," Finn said, his voice filled with determination. "We need to confront it and protect the forest."

As they approached the figure, they felt a wave of dark energy wash over them. The whispers of the forest grew frantic, urging them to stand strong and protect its magic.

The dark figure laughed, its voice a chilling echo that sent shivers down their spines. "Foolish mortals," it sneered. "You dare to challenge me? I am the Shadow King, and I will consume the Whispering Forest. You cannot stop me."

Elara and Finn stepped forward, their hearts filled with a mixture of fear and determination. They knew that they had to stand against the Shadow King and protect the forest, no matter the cost.

"We will not let you corrupt the forest's magic," Elara said, her voice steady and resolute. "We will stand against you and protect the Whispering Forest."

The Shadow King's eyes narrowed, and a malevolent smile played at the corners of his lips. "Very well," he said. "If you wish to fight, then so be it. But know this: I will show no mercy."

With a wave of his hand, the Shadow King summoned a horde of dark creatures from the depths of the forest. These twisted beings, formed from shadows and nightmares, surged forward, their eyes glowing with a malevolent light.

Elara, Finn, Rowan, and Thistle stood their ground, their hearts filled with determination. They knew that this battle would be fierce, but they were ready to fight alongside their new allies to protect the forest.

The first wave of dark creatures lunged at them, their twisted forms moving with unnatural speed. Elara and Finn fought side by side, their movements synchronized and fluid. They had trained together for this moment, and their bond was unbreakable.

Rowan's powerful strikes sent the creatures reeling, while Thistle's agility and quick thinking allowed her to outmaneuver their attacks. Vixen and Max darted in and out of the fray, their sharp teeth and claws tearing through the dark creatures with ease.

Despite their efforts, the dark creatures seemed endless, and the battle raged on. The air was filled with the sounds of clashing weapons and the cries of the wounded. The Shadow King watched from the edge of the clearing, his eyes gleaming with malevolent satisfaction.

"You cannot win," he taunted. "My power is limitless. The forest will be mine."

Elara and Finn refused to give in. They knew that the forest's magic was counting on them, and they drew strength from the whispers that filled their minds.

"We have to find the Shadow King's weakness," Finn said, his voice filled with determination. "There must be a way to defeat him."

Elara nodded, her eyes scanning the battlefield. "The forest has guided us this far," she said. "We need to trust in its wisdom and our own strength. We can find a way to defeat him."

As they continued to fight, Elara felt a strange sensation wash over her. It was as if the forest itself was speaking to her, guiding her movements and filling her with a sense of purpose.

"Elara, Finn, listen," a voice whispered in her mind. "The Shadow King draws his power from the darkness. You must find a way to sever his connection to the shadows."

Elara's eyes widened with realization. "The Silver Leaf," she said. "It holds the essence of the forest's magic. We can use it to weaken the Shadow King and sever his connection to the darkness."

Finn nodded, his eyes filled with determination. "We need to get close to him and use the Silver Leaf," he said. "It's our only chance."

With renewed resolve, Elara and Finn fought their way through the horde of dark creatures, their eyes fixed on the Shadow King. Rowan and Thistle covered their flanks, ensuring that no creature could impede their progress.

As they neared the Shadow King, the air grew colder and filled with a sense of impending doom. The dark energy emanating from him was almost overwhelming, but Elara and Finn pressed on, their hearts filled with determination.

"Foolish mortals," the Shadow King sneered. "You think you can defeat me? Your efforts are in vain."

Elara ignored his taunts, her mind focused on the task at hand. She reached into her pouch and pulled out the wooden box containing the Silver Leaf. The leaf glowed with an ethereal light, filling the air with a sense of calm and clarity.

"Now, Finn," Elara said, her voice steady. "We need to use the Silver Leaf to sever his connection to the darkness."

Finn nodded, his eyes fixed on the Shadow King. "We can do this," he said. "Together."

With a deep breath, Elara held up the Silver Leaf, its light growing brighter and more intense. The Shadow King recoiled, his eyes narrowing with rage.

"No!" he roared. "You cannot use that against me!"

Elara and Finn focused their minds, drawing on the wisdom and strength of the forest. The Silver Leaf pulsed with a powerful energy, and a beam of light shot out, striking the Shadow King.

The dark energy around him began to waver, and the creatures he had summoned faltered, their forms flickering like shadows in the wind.

"You cannot defeat me!" the Shadow King cried, his voice filled with desperation. "I am eternal!"

Elara and Finn pressed on, their determination unwavering. The light from the Silver Leaf grew brighter, enveloping the Shadow King and severing his connection to the darkness.

With a final, agonized scream, the Shadow King was consumed by the light. His form disintegrated, and the dark energy that had surrounded him dissipated, leaving the clearing bathed in the soft glow of the Silver Leaf.

The horde of dark creatures vanished, their twisted forms dissolving into the shadows from which they had come. The air grew still, and the whispers of the forest filled their minds with a sense of calm and relief.

"We did it," Elara said, her voice filled with awe. "We defeated the Shadow King."

Finn nodded, his eyes filled with gratitude. "The Silver Leaf's magic was the key," he said. "We couldn't have done it without the forest's guidance."

Rowan and Thistle approached, their faces filled with pride and relief. "You both fought with incredible courage and determination," Rowan said. "The forest is safe, thanks to you."

Thistle's eyes sparkled with excitement. "The battle was fierce, but we stood strong together," she said. "We protected the Whispering Forest."

As they stood in the clearing, the whispers of the forest grew louder, filling their minds with a sense of gratitude and approval. The trees rustled softly, and the air was filled with the scent of blooming flowers and fresh earth.

"You have proven yourselves worthy guardians of the forest," the whispers said. "The darkness has been defeated, and the balance has been restored. The forest's magic will endure for generations to come."

Elara and Finn felt a deep sense of fulfillment and pride. They had faced their greatest challenge and emerged victorious, protecting the forest and its magic.

"We couldn't have done it without each other and the forest's guidance," Elara said, her voice filled with gratitude. "We are stronger together."

Finn nodded, his eyes filled with determination. "The forest's magic is powerful, but it needs protectors," he said. "We will continue to stand guard and ensure that its wisdom and beauty are preserved."

Rowan and Thistle smiled, their hearts filled with a sense of purpose and unity. "We are all guardians of the Whispering Forest," Rowan said. "Together, we will protect it and keep its magic alive."

With renewed hope and strength, Elara, Finn, Rowan, and Thistle set out to continue their journey. They knew that their quest was far from over, but they were ready to face whatever challenges lay ahead. The forest's whispers guided them, filling their minds with a sense of purpose and clarity.

As they ventured deeper into the heart of the forest, they felt a deep connection to the land and its magic. The trees seemed to welcome them, their branches swaying gently in the breeze. The air was filled with the sounds of birds singing and leaves rustling, creating a symphony of nature's beauty.

Elara and Finn walked side by side, their bond stronger than ever. They had discovered hidden strengths within themselves, drawn from the forest's magic and their own determination.

"We have come a long way," Elara said, her voice filled with pride. "But our journey is not over. We must continue to protect the forest and uncover its secrets."

Finn nodded, his eyes filled with resolve. "We will face whatever challenges come our way," he said. "Together, we are unstoppable."

Rowan and Thistle walked behind them, their hearts filled with a sense of purpose and unity. They knew that they were part of something greater, protectors of a magical realm that held endless beauty and wisdom.

As they continued their journey, the whispers of the forest guided them, filling their minds with a sense of calm and clarity. They knew that the path ahead would be fraught with danger and deception, but they were ready to face whatever obstacles lay in their path.

Their adventure was far from over, but they faced it with courage and determination. The Battle of Shadows had given them new allies and powerful tools, and they were stronger for it. Together, they would protect the Whispering Forest and ensure that its magic and wisdom would endure for generations to come.

# Chapter 12: The Silver Leaf

The journey through the Whispering Forest had been long and arduous, filled with trials and tribulations that tested the strength and determination of Elara, Finn, Rowan, and Thistle. Their bond had grown unbreakable, and they had proven themselves time and again. Now, they were on the brink of their ultimate goal: obtaining the Silver Leaf. The whispers of the forest guided them to the location of this powerful artifact, promising them the ability to communicate with the forest and protect its ancient magic.

The air was crisp and cool as they set out that morning. The forest was alive with the sounds of birds singing and leaves rustling in the gentle breeze. The sun filtered through the dense canopy, casting dappled shadows on the forest floor. Vixen and Max trotted ahead, their senses alert for any signs of danger.

As they walked, Rowan spoke of the final test they would face. His deep voice carried a tone of reverence and solemnity, captivating his companions.

"The Silver Leaf is a powerful artifact," Rowan began. "It holds the essence of the forest's magic and the wisdom of the guardian spirits. To obtain it, we must prove ourselves worthy through one final test. This test will challenge our courage, our intelligence, and our bond with the forest."

Elara and Finn listened intently, their hearts filled with a mixture of anticipation and resolve. They knew that this final test would be their most difficult challenge yet, but they were ready to face it together.

"We have faced many trials and grown stronger with each one," Elara said, her voice steady. "We are ready for this final test. We will prove ourselves worthy of the Silver Leaf."

Thistle's eyes sparkled with determination. "The forest has guided us this far," she said. "We must trust in its wisdom and our own strength. We can obtain the Silver Leaf and protect the Whispering Forest."

As they continued their journey, the whispers of the forest grew louder, urging them forward. The path led them to a secluded glade, bathed in the soft glow of the moonlight. In the center of the glade stood a tall, ancient tree with silver leaves that shimmered in the breeze. The tree exuded an aura of wisdom and strength, and its presence filled the glade with a sense of calm and tranquility.

"This is the tree from the vision," Elara said, her voice filled with awe. "The tree that holds the Silver Leaf."

As they approached the tree, they felt a deep, resonant energy emanating from its trunk and branches. The whispers of the forest grew louder, filling their minds with a sense of calm and clarity. They knew that they were in the right place, and that the tree held the key to unlocking the magic of the Silver Leaf.

"The runes on the tree must hold the key to unlocking its magic," Rowan said, his voice filled with determination. "We need to decipher the runes and speak the words that will unlock the magic of the tree."

Elara, Finn, Rowan, and Thistle examined the runes, their minds working to decipher their meaning. The runes were written in an ancient language, and they knew that they held the key to unlocking the tree's magic.

"The runes speak of balance and harmony, of light and dark," Elara said thoughtfully. "We need to find the right words to activate the tree's magic."

Rowan nodded, his eyes scanning the runes for any clues. "The tree is a guardian of the forest's wisdom," he said. "We need to speak the words of truth and purity to unlock its magic."

Thistle's eyes sparkled with excitement. "I recognize some of these runes," she said. "They speak of the ancient magic of the forest, of the balance between light and dark. We need to trust in the wisdom of the forest and speak the words that our hearts hold."

Elara and Finn joined hands, focusing their minds and hearts on the runes. They drew on the wisdom and strength of the forest, speaking the words that their hearts held.

"Ancient tree, guardian of the Silver Leaf's magic," Elara began, her voice steady and clear. "We seek the guidance and protection of the forest. We have come with pure intent and open hearts. Show us the way."

As Elara spoke the words, the runes began to glow with a soft, blue light. The ground beneath their feet seemed to hum with energy, and the tree's branches swayed gently, as if acknowledging their words.

"You have spoken the words of truth and purity," a deep, resonant voice said. "You have proven yourselves worthy of the Silver Leaf's magic. But before you can obtain it, you must face one final test."

The air grew colder, and the glade was suddenly enveloped in a thick mist. The whispers of the forest grew urgent, filling their minds with a sense of impending challenge.

"To obtain the Silver Leaf, you must confront your deepest fears and insecurities," the voice continued. "Only by overcoming these inner demons can you prove yourselves worthy of the Silver Leaf's power."

Elara and Finn exchanged determined glances, their hearts filled with resolve. They knew that this final test would be their most difficult challenge yet, but they were ready to face it together.

"We are ready," Elara said, her voice steady. "We will confront our fears and prove ourselves worthy of the Silver Leaf."

The mist thickened, and the glade seemed to shift and change. The ancient tree with the silver leaves faded from view, replaced by a series of shadowy figures that emerged from the mist. These figures were dark and twisted, their forms shifting and changing as they approached.

Elara and Finn stood their ground, their hearts pounding with anticipation. They knew that these shadowy figures represented their deepest fears and insecurities, and they would have to confront them head-on.

The first figure lunged at Elara, its eyes glowing with a malevolent light. Elara felt a wave of fear wash over her, but she stood her ground, drawing on the strength and wisdom of the forest.

"You are not real," Elara said, her voice steady. "You are a manifestation of my fears, and I will not let you control me."

The shadowy figure hesitated, its form wavering. Elara took a deep breath and focused her mind, drawing on the calm and clarity of the forest's whispers.

"I am stronger than my fears," Elara said, her voice filled with determination. "I will overcome you and prove myself worthy of the Silver Leaf."

With a final, determined effort, Elara reached out and touched the shadowy figure. It dissolved into the mist, its malevolent light fading away. Elara felt a sense of relief and empowerment wash over her, knowing that she had confronted and overcome her fear.

Finn faced his own shadowy figure, its eyes filled with a cold, calculating light. He felt a wave of doubt and insecurity wash over him, but he stood his ground, drawing on the strength and wisdom of the forest.

"You are not real," Finn said, his voice steady. "You are a manifestation of my insecurities, and I will not let you control me."

The shadowy figure hesitated, its form wavering. Finn took a deep breath and focused his mind, drawing on the calm and clarity of the forest's whispers.

"I am stronger than my insecurities," Finn said, his voice filled with determination. "I will overcome you and prove myself worthy of the Silver Leaf."

With a final, determined effort, Finn reached out and touched the shadowy figure. It dissolved into the mist, its cold, calculating light fading away. Finn felt a sense of relief and empowerment wash over him, knowing that he had confronted and overcome his insecurities.

Rowan and Thistle faced their own shadowy figures, each confronting their deepest fears and insecurities. They drew on the strength and wisdom of the forest, standing strong and determined against the dark manifestations. One by one, they overcame their fears, proving themselves worthy of the Silver Leaf's power.

As the final shadowy figure dissolved into the mist, the air grew warmer, and the ancient tree with the silver leaves reappeared in the glade. The whispers of the forest filled their minds with a sense of approval and gratitude.

"You have proven yourselves worthy," the deep, resonant voice said. "You have confronted your deepest fears and insecurities, and you have emerged victorious. You are now ready to obtain the Silver Leaf and unlock its power."

The ancient tree began to shimmer and glow with an ethereal light. A small, intricately carved wooden box appeared at the base of the tree, its surface covered in ancient runes.

"This box contains the Silver Leaf," the voice said. "It holds the essence of the forest's magic and the wisdom of the guardian spirits. Use it wisely and with respect."

Elara and Finn stepped forward, their hearts filled with gratitude and determination. They carefully picked up the wooden box, feeling its smooth surface and the warmth of its magic.

"Thank you, guardian," Elara said, her voice filled with gratitude. "We will use the Silver Leaf to protect the forest and continue our quest."

The voice smiled, its presence filling the glade with a sense of approval. "You have earned my respect and my guidance," it said. "The path to the heart of the forest lies before you. Follow the whispers and trust in the wisdom of the forest. You are ready to face whatever challenges lie ahead."

With renewed hope and strength, Elara, Finn, Rowan, and Thistle set out on the next leg of their journey, guided by the whispers and the wisdom of the forest. They knew that the path ahead would be fraught with danger and deception, but they were ready to face whatever obstacles lay in their path.

As they ventured deeper into the forest, they felt a deep connection to the land and its magic. The trees seemed to welcome them, their branches swaying gently in the breeze. The air was filled with the sounds of birds singing and leaves rustling, creating a symphony of nature's beauty.

Elara and Finn walked side by side, their bond stronger than ever. They had discovered hidden strengths within themselves, drawn from the forest's magic and their own determination.

"We have come a long way," Elara said, her voice filled with pride. "But our journey is not over. We must continue to protect the forest and uncover its secrets."

Finn nodded, his eyes filled with resolve. "We will face whatever challenges come our way," he said. "Together, we are unstoppable."

Rowan and Thistle walked behind them, their hearts filled with a sense of purpose and unity. They knew that they were part of something greater, protectors of a magical realm that held endless beauty and wisdom.

As they continued their journey, the whispers of the forest guided them, filling their minds with a sense of calm and clarity. They knew that the path ahead would be fraught with danger and deception, but they were ready to face whatever obstacles lay in their path.

Their adventure was far from over, but they faced it with courage and determination. The final test to obtain the Silver Leaf had given them new allies and powerful tools, and they were stronger for it. Together, they would protect the Whispering Forest and ensure that its magic and wisdom would endure for generations to come.

The glade with the ancient tree and the Silver Leaf had revealed to them the true essence of their quest. It was not just about obtaining the Silver Leaf but about discovering the strength within themselves and their bond with the forest. They had proven their worthiness, and now, with the Silver Leaf in their possession, they had the power to communicate with the forest and protect it from any threat.

As they ventured deeper into the heart of the forest, the whispers grew clearer, guiding them toward their ultimate goal. They knew that their journey was far from over, but with the Silver Leaf's magic and the forest's wisdom, they felt ready to face whatever challenges lay ahead.

Elara, Finn, Rowan, and Thistle walked with renewed determination, their hearts filled with a sense of purpose and unity. The forest had chosen them as its protectors, and they were ready to fulfill that role with courage and dedication.

The path ahead was uncertain, but they knew that as long as they trusted in the forest's wisdom and their own strength, they could overcome any obstacle. Together, they would protect the Whispering Forest and ensure that its magic and beauty would endure for generations to come.

Their adventure was far from over, but they faced it with courage and determination. The final test to obtain the Silver Leaf had given them new allies and powerful tools, and they were stronger for it. Together, they would protect the Whispering Forest and ensure that its magic and wisdom would endure for generations to come.

As they continued their journey, they felt a deep connection to the land and its magic. The trees seemed to welcome them, their branches swaying gently in the breeze. The air was filled with the sounds of birds singing and leaves rustling, creating a symphony of nature's beauty.

Elara and Finn walked side by side, their bond stronger than ever. They had discovered hidden strengths within themselves, drawn from the forest's magic and their own determination.

"We have come a long way," Elara said, her voice filled with pride. "But our journey is not over. We must continue to protect the forest and uncover its secrets."

Finn nodded, his eyes filled with resolve. "We will face whatever challenges come our way," he said. "Together, we are unstoppable."

Rowan and Thistle walked behind them, their hearts filled with a sense of purpose and unity. They knew that they were part of something greater, protectors of a magical realm that held endless beauty and wisdom.

As they continued their journey, the whispers of the forest guided them, filling their minds with a sense of calm and clarity. They knew that the path ahead would be fraught with danger and deception, but they were ready to face whatever obstacles lay in their path.

Their adventure was far from over, but they faced it with courage and determination. The final test to obtain the Silver Leaf had given them new allies and powerful tools, and they were stronger for it. Together, they would protect the Whispering Forest and ensure that its magic and wisdom would endure for generations to come.

The glade with the ancient tree and the Silver Leaf had revealed to them the true essence of their quest. It was not just about obtaining the Silver Leaf but about discovering the strength within themselves and their bond with the forest. They had proven their worthiness, and now, with the Silver Leaf in their possession, they had the power to communicate with the forest and protect it from any threat.

As they ventured deeper into the heart of the forest, the whispers grew clearer, guiding them toward their ultimate goal. They knew that their journey was far from over, but with the Silver Leaf's magic and the forest's wisdom, they felt ready to face whatever challenges lay ahead.

Elara, Finn, Rowan, and Thistle walked with renewed determination, their hearts filled with a sense of purpose and unity. The forest had chosen them as its protectors, and they were ready to fulfill that role with courage and dedication.

The path ahead was uncertain, but they knew that as long as they trusted in the forest's wisdom and their own strength, they could overcome any obstacle. Together, they would protect the Whispering Forest and ensure that its magic and beauty would endure for generations to come.

Their adventure was far from over, but they faced it with courage and determination. The final test to obtain the Silver Leaf had given them new allies and powerful tools, and they were stronger for it. Together, they would protect the Whispering Forest and ensure that its magic and wisdom would endure for generations to come.

The glade with the ancient tree and the Silver Leaf had revealed to them the true essence of their quest. It was not just about obtaining the Silver Leaf but about discovering the strength within themselves and their bond with the forest. They had proven their worthiness, and now, with the Silver Leaf in their possession, they had the power to communicate with the forest and protect it from any threat.

As they ventured deeper into the heart of the forest, the whispers grew clearer, guiding them toward their ultimate goal. They knew that their journey was far from over, but with the Silver Leaf's magic and the forest's wisdom, they felt ready to face whatever challenges lay ahead.

Elara, Finn, Rowan, and Thistle walked with renewed determination, their hearts filled with a sense of purpose and unity. The forest had chosen them as its protectors, and they were ready to fulfill that role with courage and dedication.

The path ahead was uncertain, but they knew that as long as they trusted in the forest's wisdom and their own strength, they could overcome any obstacle. Together, they would protect the Whispering Forest and ensure that its magic and beauty would endure for generations to come.

# Chapter 13: The Return of the Lost Prince

The journey through the Whispering Forest had brought Elara, Finn, Rowan, and Thistle closer than ever to uncovering its deepest secrets. They had faced trials and tribulations, each more challenging than the last, and had proven their worthiness by obtaining the Silver Leaf. But one mystery still eluded them—the fate of the Lost Prince, Aldric. Guided by the whispers of the forest, they set out to follow the clues that would lead them to him and uncover the role he played in the forest's history and future.

The morning air was cool and crisp as they set out. The forest was alive with the sounds of birds singing and leaves rustling in the gentle breeze. The sun filtered through the dense canopy, casting dappled shadows on the forest floor. Vixen and Max trotted ahead, their senses alert for any signs of danger.

As they walked, Rowan spoke of the clues they had gathered about the Lost Prince. His deep voice carried a tone of reverence and solemnity, captivating his companions.

"Prince Aldric was a brave and compassionate leader," Rowan began. "He ventured into the Whispering Forest centuries ago to seek the counsel of the guardian spirits but was never seen again. We know that he was lost, but we also believe that he may have been placed under a magical curse."

Elara and Finn listened intently, their hearts filled with a mixture of anticipation and resolve. They knew that finding the Lost Prince could hold the key to protecting the forest and uncovering its secrets.

"The forest has guided us this far," Elara said, her voice steady. "We must trust in its wisdom and our own strength. We can find the Lost Prince and free him from the curse."

Thistle's eyes sparkled with determination. "If we can reunite him with his people, it could change everything," she said. "We need to follow the clues and see where they lead."

As they continued their journey, the whispers of the forest grew louder, urging them forward. The path led them to a secluded glade, bathed in the soft glow of the moonlight. In the center of the glade stood a tall, ancient tree with bark that seemed to shimmer with an ethereal light. The tree exuded an aura of wisdom and strength, and its presence filled the glade with a sense of calm and tranquility.

"This tree is special," Elara said, her voice filled with awe. "I can feel its power. It must be connected to the Lost Prince."

Rowan nodded, his eyes scanning the tree for any signs of a hidden message. "The tree may hold clues that can help us find the prince," he said. "We need to look closely."

As they approached the tree, they noticed a series of intricate carvings etched into its bark. The carvings depicted scenes from Prince Aldric's life, from his early years as a young prince to his journey into the Whispering Forest. Each image was detailed and lifelike, telling the story of a brave and compassionate leader.

Finn traced his fingers over the carvings, feeling a sense of connection to the Lost Prince. "These carvings are like a record of his life," he said. "But there's something more here. Look at this."

He pointed to a section of the tree where the carvings seemed to form a pattern, creating a series of symbols and runes. The runes pulsed with a faint, blue light, as if holding a hidden message.

Elara examined the runes closely, her mind working to decipher their meaning. "The runes speak of a hidden path," she said. "A path that leads to where the prince may still be alive. We need to follow these clues and find the hidden path."

Thistle's eyes sparkled with excitement. "This could be the key to finding Prince Aldric," she said. "We should follow the runes and see where they lead."

Rowan nodded in agreement. "The forest is guiding us," he said. "We must trust in its wisdom and continue our journey."

With renewed determination, Elara, Finn, Rowan, and Thistle set out to follow the clues left by the runes. The whispers of the forest guided them, filling their minds with a sense of purpose and clarity. They knew that the journey ahead would be challenging, but they were ready to face whatever obstacles lay in their path.

As they ventured deeper into the forest, the runes led them to a series of hidden landmarks and ancient relics. Each clue brought them closer to uncovering the truth about Prince Aldric's fate. They navigated treacherous terrain, crossed rushing rivers, and faced cunning creatures that sought to impede their progress. But with each trial, their bond grew stronger, and their determination never wavered.

One particularly difficult challenge came in the form of a dense, shadowy thicket that seemed to block their path. The thicket was filled with twisted vines and thorny bushes, creating a nearly impenetrable barrier. The whispers of the forest urged them to find a way through, but the path seemed impossible.

"We need to find a way around this thicket," Finn said, his voice filled with determination. "The prince must be on the other side."

Rowan examined the thicket, his eyes scanning for any sign of a hidden path. "There must be a way through," he said. "We just need to find it."

Thistle darted ahead, her nimble form easily navigating the tangled vines. "I think I see something," she called out, pointing to a narrow gap in the thicket.

Elara and Finn followed Thistle, carefully making their way through the narrow gap. The vines scratched at their skin and clothing, but they pressed on, determined to reach the other side. Vixen and Max stayed close, their senses alert for any signs of danger.

After what felt like hours of struggling through the thicket, they finally emerged into a small clearing. The clearing was bathed in the soft glow of the moonlight, and in the center stood a tall, ancient tree with dark, shadowy leaves that seemed to absorb the light. The tree swayed gently, its branches forming a natural canopy that cast dappled shadows on the ground.

"This must be the place," Finn said, his voice filled with awe. "The place where the prince is hidden."

As they approached the tree, they felt a deep, resonant energy emanating from its trunk and branches. The whispers of the forest grew louder, filling their minds with a sense of calm and clarity. They knew that they were in the right place, and that the tree held the key to unlocking the magical curse that bound the prince.

"The runes on the tree must hold the key to unlocking the curse," Rowan said, his voice filled with determination. "We need to decipher the runes and speak the words that will free the prince."

Elara, Finn, Rowan, and Thistle examined the runes, their minds working to decipher their meaning. The runes were written in an ancient language, and they knew that they held the key to unlocking the tree's magic.

"The runes speak of balance and harmony, of light and dark," Elara said thoughtfully. "We need to find the right words to activate the tree's magic and free the prince from the curse."

Rowan nodded, his eyes scanning the runes for any clues. "The tree is a guardian of the forest's wisdom," he said. "We need to speak the words of truth and purity to unlock its magic."

Thistle's eyes sparkled with excitement. "I recognize some of these runes," she said. "They speak of the ancient magic of the forest, of the balance between light and dark. We need to trust in the wisdom of the forest and speak the words that our hearts hold."

Elara and Finn joined hands, focusing their minds and hearts on the runes. They drew on the wisdom and strength of the forest, speaking the words that their hearts held.

"Ancient tree, guardian of the prince's magic," Elara began, her voice steady and clear. "We seek the guidance and protection of the forest. We have come with pure intent and open hearts. Show us the way."

As Elara spoke the words, the runes began to glow with a soft, blue light. The ground beneath their feet seemed to hum with energy, and the tree's branches swayed gently, as if acknowledging their words.

"You have spoken the words of truth and purity," a deep, resonant voice said. "You have proven yourselves worthy of freeing the prince. The magical curse that binds him will now be lifted."

The tree's dark, shadowy leaves began to shimmer and glow with an ethereal light. A small, intricately carved wooden box appeared at the base of the tree, its surface covered in ancient runes.

"This box contains the key to freeing the prince," the voice said. "It holds the essence of the forest's magic and the wisdom of the guardian spirits. Use it wisely and with respect."

Elara and Finn stepped forward, their hearts filled with gratitude and determination. They carefully picked up the wooden box, feeling its smooth surface and the warmth of its magic.

"Thank you, guardian," Elara said, her voice filled with gratitude. "We will use the key to free the prince and continue our quest."

The voice smiled, its presence filling the clearing with a sense of approval. "You have earned my respect and my guidance," it said. "The path to the prince lies before you. Follow the whispers and trust in the wisdom of the forest. You are ready to face whatever challenges lie ahead."

With renewed hope and strength, Elara, Finn, Rowan, and Thistle set out to find the prince. The whispers of the forest guided them, filling their minds with a sense of purpose and clarity. They knew that the journey ahead would be challenging, but they were ready to face whatever obstacles lay in their path.

As they ventured deeper into the forest, they felt a deep connection to the land and its magic. The trees seemed to welcome them, their branches swaying gently in the breeze. The air was filled with the sounds of birds singing and leaves rustling, creating a symphony of nature's beauty.

After several hours of walking, they reached a secluded cave, hidden deep within the heart of the forest. The entrance to the cave was covered in moss and vines, creating an almost impenetrable barrier. But the whispers of the forest urged them forward, and they knew that the cave held the key to freeing the prince.

"This cave must be the final clue," Finn said, his voice filled with determination. "We need to find a way inside."

Rowan examined the entrance to the cave, his eyes scanning for any signs of a hidden passage. "There must be a way to open the entrance," he said. "The clues we've found so far must hold the key."

Thistle darted ahead, her nimble form easily navigating the tangled vines. "I think I see something," she called out, pointing to a series of runes carved into the rock.

Elara and Finn followed Thistle, carefully examining the runes. The runes pulsed with a faint, blue light, as if holding a hidden message.

"The runes speak of balance and harmony, of light and dark," Elara said thoughtfully. "We need to find the right words to activate the cave's magic and free the prince."

Rowan nodded in agreement. "The cave is a guardian of the forest's wisdom," he said. "We need to speak the words of truth and purity to unlock its magic."

Elara and Finn joined hands, focusing their minds and hearts on the runes. They drew on the wisdom and strength of the forest, speaking the words that their hearts held.

"Ancient cave, guardian of the prince's magic," Elara began, her voice steady and clear. "We seek the guidance and protection of the forest. We have come with pure intent and open hearts. Show us the way."

As Elara spoke the words, the runes began to glow with a soft, blue light. The ground beneath their feet seemed to hum with energy, and the entrance to the cave slowly began to open, revealing a hidden passage that led deeper into the cave.

"We did it," Finn said, his voice filled with triumph. "The path is open. We need to continue following the clues."

As they ventured deeper into the cave, the air grew cooler and filled with an otherworldly energy. The walls of the cave were covered in intricate carvings and runes, telling the story of Prince Aldric's journey into the forest. Each image was detailed and lifelike, creating a vivid record of the prince's life.

At the end of the passage, they reached a small, hidden chamber. In the center of the chamber stood a tall, imposing figure draped in dark, flowing robes. His hair was long and black, and his eyes glowed with an otherworldly light. He exuded an aura of power and mystery, and his presence filled the chamber with a sense of tension and anticipation.

"Welcome, travelers," the figure said, his voice like the rustle of leaves in the wind. "I am Aldric, the Lost Prince of the Whispering Forest. I have been waiting for you."

Elara and Finn stepped forward, their hearts filled with a mixture of fear and determination. They had uncovered the truth about the Lost Prince, and they were ready to face whatever challenges lay ahead.

"We seek your guidance and protection," Elara said, her voice steady. "We are on a quest to protect the Whispering Forest and uncover its secrets. We need your help to continue our journey."

Aldric's eyes narrowed, and a faint smile played at the corners of his lips. "Many have come seeking my guidance and protection," he said. "But few have proven themselves worthy. You must face my trials and earn my respect before I will grant you my aid."

Finn stepped forward, his eyes blazing with determination. "We are ready to face your trials," he said. "We will do whatever it takes to protect the forest."

Aldric's smile widened, and he raised his hands, casting a series of intricate spells. The air around them shimmered with magic, and the chamber was transformed into a labyrinth of twisting paths and hidden dangers.

"Your first trial is a test of courage and resolve," Aldric said. "You must navigate this labyrinth and reach the heart of the chamber. Only then will you prove yourselves worthy of my guidance."

Elara, Finn, Rowan, and Thistle nodded, their hearts filled with determination. They knew that the labyrinth would be filled with challenges, but they were ready to face whatever obstacles lay ahead.

As they entered the labyrinth, the paths twisted and turned, creating a disorienting maze of rock and shadows. The air was thick with an otherworldly energy, and the whispers of the forest seemed to fade into the background.

"We need to stay together and trust in each other," Elara said, her voice steady. "The labyrinth is designed to test our courage and resolve. We must not lose our way."

Rowan nodded, his eyes scanning the paths for any sign of danger. "We need to keep moving and stay focused," he said. "The labyrinth is filled with traps and illusions. We must be vigilant."

Thistle darted ahead, her nimble form easily navigating the twisting paths. "I can sense the magic of the labyrinth," she said. "We need to follow the path of light. It will lead us to the heart of the chamber."

Elara and Finn followed Thistle, carefully making their way through the labyrinth. The paths were filled with hidden traps and illusions, designed to confuse and deceive them. They encountered shadowy figures that sought to block their way, but they stood their ground and pressed on, determined to reach the heart of the chamber.

As they ventured deeper into the labyrinth, they felt a growing sense of tension and anticipation. The paths grew darker and more twisted, and the air was filled with an eerie silence. They knew that they were nearing the heart of the chamber, and that the most difficult part of the trial lay ahead.

After what felt like hours of navigating the labyrinth, they reached a small clearing. In the center of the clearing stood a tall, ancient tree with dark, shadowy leaves that seemed to absorb the light. The tree swayed gently, its branches forming a natural canopy that cast dappled shadows on the ground.

"This must be the heart of the chamber," Finn said, his voice filled with awe. "We need to prove our worthiness to Aldric."

As they approached the tree, they felt a deep, resonant energy emanating from its trunk and branches. The whispers of the forest grew louder, filling their minds with a sense of calm and clarity. They knew that they were in the right place, and that the tree held the key to the next step of their journey.

Aldric appeared before them, his eyes glowing with an otherworldly light. "You have reached the heart of the chamber," he said. "But your trials are not yet over. You must face one final test to prove your worthiness."

He raised his hands, casting a powerful spell that enveloped the clearing in a shimmering light. The ground beneath their feet seemed to hum with energy, and a series of ancient runes appeared on the trunk of the tree.

"This is a test of wisdom and insight," Aldric said. "You must decipher the runes and unlock the magic of the tree. Only then will you earn my respect and receive the artifact you seek."

Elara, Finn, Rowan, and Thistle examined the runes, their minds working to decipher their meaning. The runes were written in an ancient language, and they knew that they held the key to unlocking the tree's magic.

"The runes speak of balance and harmony, of light and dark," Elara said thoughtfully. "We need to find the right words to activate the tree's magic."

Rowan nodded, his eyes scanning the runes for any clues. "The tree is a guardian of the forest's wisdom," he said. "We need to speak the words of truth and purity to unlock its magic."

Thistle's eyes sparkled with excitement. "I recognize some of these runes," she said. "They speak of the ancient magic of the forest, of the balance between light and dark. We need to trust in the wisdom of the forest and speak the words that our hearts hold."

Elara and Finn joined hands, focusing their minds and hearts on the runes. They drew on the wisdom and strength of the forest, speaking the words that their hearts held.

"Ancient tree, guardian of the chamber's wisdom," Elara began, her voice steady and clear. "We seek the guidance and protection of the forest. We have come with pure intent and open hearts. Show us the way."

As Elara spoke the words, the runes began to glow with a soft, blue light. The ground beneath their feet seemed to hum with energy, and the tree's branches swayed gently, as if acknowledging their words.

"You have spoken the words of truth and purity," Aldric said, his voice filled with approval. "You have proven yourselves worthy of my respect. I will grant you the artifact you seek."

He raised his hands, casting a spell that caused the tree to shimmer and glow with an ethereal light. A small, intricately carved wooden box appeared at the base of the tree, its surface covered in ancient runes.

"This box contains a magical artifact that will aid you on your quest," Aldric said. "It holds the essence of the chamber's magic, a powerful tool that will help you protect the forest and stand against the darkness. Use it wisely and with respect."

Elara and Finn stepped forward, their hearts filled with gratitude and determination. They carefully picked up the wooden box, feeling its smooth surface and the warmth of its magic.

"Thank you, Aldric," Elara said, her voice filled with gratitude. "We will use the artifact to protect the forest and continue our quest."

Aldric smiled, his eyes twinkling with approval. "You have earned my respect and my guidance," he said. "The path to the heart of the forest lies before you. Follow the whispers and trust in the wisdom of the forest. You are ready to face whatever challenges lie ahead."

With renewed hope and strength, Elara, Finn, Rowan, and Thistle set out on the next leg of their journey, guided by the whispers and the wisdom of the forest. They knew that the path ahead would be fraught with danger and deception, but they were ready to face whatever obstacles lay in their path.

As they ventured deeper into the forest, they encountered a series of trials and challenges that tested their courage, intelligence, and bond with the land. They navigated treacherous terrain, crossed rushing rivers, and faced cunning creatures that sought to impede their progress. But with each trial, their bond grew stronger, and their determination never wavered.

Their adventure was far from over, but they faced it with courage and determination. The encounter with Aldric, the Lost Prince, had given them new allies and powerful tools, and they were stronger for it. Together, they would protect the Whispering Forest and ensure that its magic and wisdom would endure for generations to come.

As they continued their journey, they felt a deep connection to the land and its magic. The trees seemed to welcome them, their branches swaying gently in the breeze. The air was filled with the sounds of birds singing and leaves rustling, creating a symphony of nature's beauty.

Elara and Finn walked side by side, their bond stronger than ever. They had discovered hidden strengths within themselves, drawn from the forest's magic and their own determination.

"We have come a long way," Elara said, her voice filled with pride. "But our journey is not over. We must continue to protect the forest and uncover its secrets."

Finn nodded, his eyes filled with resolve. "We will face whatever challenges come our way," he said. "Together, we are unstoppable."

Rowan and Thistle walked behind them, their hearts filled with a sense of purpose and unity. They knew that they were part of something greater, protectors of a magical realm that held endless beauty and wisdom.

As they continued their journey, the whispers of the forest guided them, filling their minds with a sense of calm and clarity. They knew that the path ahead would be fraught with danger and deception, but they were ready to face whatever obstacles lay in their path.

Their adventure was far from over, but they faced it with courage and determination. The final test to obtain the Silver Leaf had given them new allies and powerful tools, and they were stronger for it. Together, they would protect the Whispering Forest and ensure that its magic and wisdom would endure for generations to come.

The glade with the ancient tree and the Silver Leaf had revealed to them the true essence of their quest. It was not just about obtaining the Silver Leaf but about discovering the strength within themselves and their bond with the forest. They had proven their worthiness, and now, with the Silver Leaf in their possession, they had the power to communicate with the forest and protect it from any threat.

As they ventured deeper into the heart of the forest, the whispers grew clearer, guiding them toward their ultimate goal. They knew that their journey was far from over, but with the Silver Leaf's magic and the forest's wisdom, they felt ready to face whatever challenges lay ahead.

Elara, Finn, Rowan, and Thistle walked with renewed determination, their hearts filled with a sense of purpose and unity. The forest had chosen them as its protectors, and they were ready to fulfill that role with courage and dedication.

The path ahead was uncertain, but they knew that as long as they trusted in the forest's wisdom and their own strength, they could overcome any obstacle. Together, they would protect the Whispering Forest and ensure that its magic and beauty would endure for generations to come.

Their adventure was far from over, but they faced it with courage and determination. The final test to obtain the Silver Leaf had given them new allies and powerful tools, and they were stronger for it. Together, they would protect the Whispering Forest and ensure that its magic and wisdom would endure for generations to come.

The glade with the ancient tree and the Silver Leaf had revealed to them the true essence of their quest. It was not just about obtaining the Silver Leaf but about discovering the strength within themselves and their bond with the forest. They had proven their worthiness, and now, with the Silver Leaf in their possession, they had the power to communicate with the forest and protect it from any threat.

As they ventured deeper into the heart of the forest, the whispers grew clearer, guiding them toward their ultimate goal. They knew that their journey was far from over, but with the Silver Leaf's magic and the forest's wisdom, they felt ready to face whatever challenges lay ahead.

Elara, Finn, Rowan, and Thistle walked with renewed determination, their hearts filled with a sense of purpose and unity. The forest had chosen them as its protectors, and they were ready to fulfill that role with courage and dedication.

The path ahead was uncertain, but they knew that as long as they trusted in the forest's wisdom and their own strength, they could overcome any obstacle. Together, they would protect the Whispering Forest and ensure that its magic and beauty would endure for generations to come.

# Chapter 14: The Whispering Prophecy

Elara, Finn, Rowan, and Thistle had traversed the Whispering Forest, facing trials and gaining wisdom from the ancient land. With the Silver Leaf in their possession and the guidance of the Lost Prince, they had come to understand their role as protectors of the forest. However, one final mystery remained—a prophecy that foretold the future of the Whispering Forest. Uncovering this prophecy would reveal their ultimate challenge and prepare them for the final test that would determine the fate of the forest.

The morning air was filled with anticipation as they set out. The forest seemed to sense the importance of their quest, the trees whispering secrets that only those truly attuned to the land could hear. Vixen and Max stayed close, their keen senses on alert as they guided their human companions through the dense foliage.

Rowan spoke of the prophecy that had long been rumored among the guardians of the forest. His deep voice resonated with a sense of urgency and reverence, drawing his companions' attention.

"The Whispering Prophecy is said to be the forest's most closely guarded secret," Rowan began. "It foretells the future of the Whispering Forest and the fate of its guardians. The prophecy has been hidden for centuries, known only to a select few. To uncover it, we must prove ourselves worthy once more."

Elara and Finn listened intently, their hearts filled with a mixture of curiosity and resolve. They knew that finding the prophecy was crucial to understanding their role in the forest's future.

"The forest has guided us this far," Elara said, her voice steady. "We must trust in its wisdom and our own strength. We can uncover the prophecy and ensure its fulfillment."

Thistle's eyes sparkled with determination. "If we can understand the prophecy, it will guide us through the final challenge," she said. "We need to follow the clues and see where they lead."

As they continued their journey, the whispers of the forest grew louder, urging them forward. The path led them to a secluded glade, bathed in the soft glow of the moonlight. In the center of the glade stood a tall, ancient tree with bark that seemed to shimmer with an ethereal light. The tree exuded an aura of wisdom and strength, and its presence filled the glade with a sense of calm and tranquility.

"This tree is special," Elara said, her voice filled with awe. "I can feel its power. It must be connected to the prophecy."

Rowan nodded, his eyes scanning the tree for any signs of a hidden message. "The tree may hold clues that can help us find the prophecy," he said. "We need to look closely."

As they approached the tree, they noticed a series of intricate carvings etched into its bark. The carvings depicted scenes from the forest's history, from its creation to the present day. Each image was detailed and lifelike, telling the story of the forest's magic and the guardians who protected it.

Finn traced his fingers over the carvings, feeling a sense of connection to the forest. "These carvings are like a record of the forest's history," he said. "But there's something more here. Look at this."

He pointed to a section of the tree where the carvings seemed to form a pattern, creating a series of symbols and runes. The runes pulsed with a faint, blue light, as if holding a hidden message.

Elara examined the runes closely, her mind working to decipher their meaning. "The runes speak of a hidden path," she said. "A path that leads to the prophecy. We need to follow these clues and find the hidden path."

Thistle's eyes sparkled with excitement. "This could be the key to finding the prophecy," she said. "We should follow the runes and see where they lead."

Rowan nodded in agreement. "The forest is guiding us," he said. "We must trust in its wisdom and continue our journey."

With renewed determination, Elara, Finn, Rowan, and Thistle set out to follow the clues left by the runes. The whispers of the forest guided them, filling their minds with a sense of purpose and clarity. They knew that the journey ahead would be challenging, but they were ready to face whatever obstacles lay in their path.

As they ventured deeper into the forest, the runes led them to a series of hidden landmarks and ancient relics. Each clue brought them closer to uncovering the prophecy. They navigated treacherous terrain, crossed rushing rivers, and faced cunning creatures that sought to impede their progress. But with each trial, their bond grew stronger, and their determination never wavered.

One particularly difficult challenge came in the form of a dense, shadowy thicket that seemed to block their path. The thicket was filled with twisted vines and thorny bushes, creating a nearly impenetrable barrier. The whispers of the forest urged them to find a way through, but the path seemed impossible.

"We need to find a way around this thicket," Finn said, his voice filled with determination. "The prophecy must be on the other side."

Rowan examined the thicket, his eyes scanning for any sign of a hidden path. "There must be a way through," he said. "We just need to find it."

Thistle darted ahead, her nimble form easily navigating the tangled vines. "I think I see something," she called out, pointing to a narrow gap in the thicket.

Elara and Finn followed Thistle, carefully making their way through the narrow gap. The vines scratched at their skin and clothing, but they pressed on, determined to reach the other side. Vixen and Max stayed close, their senses alert for any signs of danger.

After what felt like hours of struggling through the thicket, they finally emerged into a small clearing. The clearing was bathed in the soft glow of the moonlight, and in the center stood a tall, ancient tree with dark, shadowy leaves that seemed to absorb the light. The tree swayed gently, its branches forming a natural canopy that cast dappled shadows on the ground.

"This must be the place," Finn said, his voice filled with awe. "The place where the prophecy is hidden."

As they approached the tree, they felt a deep, resonant energy emanating from its trunk and branches. The whispers of the forest grew louder, filling their minds with a sense of calm and clarity. They knew that they were in the right place, and that the tree held the key to unlocking the prophecy.

"The runes on the tree must hold the key to unlocking the prophecy," Rowan said, his voice filled with determination. "We need to decipher the runes and speak the words that will reveal the prophecy."

Elara, Finn, Rowan, and Thistle examined the runes, their minds working to decipher their meaning. The runes were written in an ancient language, and they knew that they held the key to unlocking the tree's magic.

"The runes speak of balance and harmony, of light and dark," Elara said thoughtfully. "We need to find the right words to activate the tree's magic and reveal the prophecy."

Rowan nodded, his eyes scanning the runes for any clues. "The tree is a guardian of the forest's wisdom," he said. "We need to speak the words of truth and purity to unlock its magic."

Thistle's eyes sparkled with excitement. "I recognize some of these runes," she said. "They speak of the ancient magic of the forest, of the balance between light and dark. We need to trust in the wisdom of the forest and speak the words that our hearts hold."

Elara and Finn joined hands, focusing their minds and hearts on the runes. They drew on the wisdom and strength of the forest, speaking the words that their hearts held.

"Ancient tree, guardian of the prophecy's magic," Elara began, her voice steady and clear. "We seek the guidance and protection of the forest. We have come with pure intent and open hearts. Show us the way."

As Elara spoke the words, the runes began to glow with a soft, blue light. The ground beneath their feet seemed to hum with energy, and the tree's branches swayed gently, as if acknowledging their words.

"You have spoken the words of truth and purity," a deep, resonant voice said. "You have proven yourselves worthy of uncovering the prophecy. The Whispering Prophecy will now be revealed to you."

The tree's dark, shadowy leaves began to shimmer and glow with an ethereal light. A scroll appeared at the base of the tree, its surface covered in ancient runes.

"This scroll contains the Whispering Prophecy," the voice said. "It holds the essence of the forest's future and the fate of its guardians. Use it wisely and with respect."

Elara and Finn stepped forward, their hearts filled with gratitude and determination. They carefully picked up the scroll, feeling its smooth surface and the warmth of its magic.

"Thank you, guardian," Elara said, her voice filled with gratitude. "We will use the prophecy to protect the forest and continue our quest."

The voice smiled, its presence filling the clearing with a sense of approval. "You have earned my respect and my guidance," it said. "The path to fulfilling the prophecy lies before you. Follow the whispers and trust in the wisdom of the forest. You are ready to face whatever challenges lie ahead."

With renewed hope and strength, Elara, Finn, Rowan, and Thistle set out to study the prophecy and understand their role in ensuring its fulfillment. The whispers of the forest guided them, filling their minds with a sense of purpose and clarity. They knew that the journey ahead would be challenging, but they were ready to face whatever obstacles lay in their path.

As they ventured deeper into the forest, they found a secluded glade where they could unroll the scroll and study its contents. The glade was peaceful and serene, the perfect place to absorb the wisdom of the prophecy.

Elara carefully unrolled the scroll, revealing a series of intricate runes and symbols that told the story of the Whispering Forest's future. The prophecy spoke of a great darkness that would threaten the forest, but also of a group of guardians who would rise to protect it.

"The prophecy speaks of us," Finn said, his voice filled with awe. "We are the guardians who must protect the forest from the coming darkness."

Elara nodded, her eyes scanning the runes for more information. "It also speaks of a final challenge," she said. "A test that will determine the fate of the forest. We must prepare ourselves for this challenge and ensure that we are ready to face it."

Rowan's eyes were filled with determination. "The prophecy has guided us this far," he said. "We must trust in its wisdom and our own strength. We can face the final challenge and protect the forest."

Thistle's eyes sparkled with excitement. "The forest has chosen us as its protectors," she said. "We must fulfill our role and ensure the prophecy's fulfillment."

As they studied the prophecy, they realized that their journey had been leading them to this moment. The trials they had faced and the wisdom they had gained were all part of their preparation for the final challenge. They knew that the path ahead would be fraught with danger, but they were ready to face it with courage and determination.

With the Silver Leaf in their possession and the guidance of the prophecy, they set out to prepare for the final challenge. They trained tirelessly, honing their skills and deepening their connection to the forest. They knew that their bond as a group and their connection to the forest's magic would be crucial in overcoming the darkness that threatened the land.

As they trained, the whispers of the forest grew louder, filling their minds with a sense of urgency and purpose. They knew that the time for the final challenge was approaching, and they needed to be ready.

One evening, as they rested by a campfire, Elara shared her thoughts with her companions. "The prophecy speaks of a great darkness," she said, her voice filled with determination. "But it also speaks of light and hope. We are the guardians who must bring that hope to the forest."

Finn nodded, his eyes filled with resolve. "We have faced many challenges and grown stronger with each one," he said. "We are ready to face the final challenge and protect the forest."

Rowan's deep voice resonated with a sense of unity. "The forest has chosen us," he said. "We must trust in its wisdom and our own strength. Together, we can overcome any obstacle."

Thistle's eyes sparkled with excitement. "We have come a long way," she said. "But our journey is not over. We must continue to protect the forest and ensure the prophecy's fulfillment."

With renewed determination, Elara, Finn, Rowan, and Thistle set out to prepare for the final challenge. They knew that their bond as a group and their connection to the forest's magic would be crucial in overcoming the darkness that threatened the land.

As they trained, they felt a deep connection to the forest and its magic. The trees seemed to welcome them, their branches swaying gently in the breeze. The air was filled with the sounds of birds singing and leaves rustling, creating a symphony of nature's beauty.

Elara and Finn walked side by side, their bond stronger than ever. They had discovered hidden strengths within themselves, drawn from the forest's magic and their own determination.

"We have come a long way," Elara said, her voice filled with pride. "But our journey is not over. We must continue to protect the forest and uncover its secrets."

Finn nodded, his eyes filled with resolve. "We will face whatever challenges come our way," he said. "Together, we are unstoppable."

Rowan and Thistle walked behind them, their hearts filled with a sense of purpose and unity. They knew that they were part of something greater, protectors of a magical realm that held endless beauty and wisdom.

As they continued their journey, the whispers of the forest guided them, filling their minds with a sense of calm and clarity. They knew that the path ahead would be fraught with danger and deception, but they were ready to face whatever obstacles lay in their path.

One day, as they trained in a secluded glade, the whispers of the forest grew urgent, filling their minds with a sense of impending challenge. They knew that the time for the final test was approaching, and they needed to be ready.

"The prophecy speaks of a final challenge," Elara said, her voice filled with determination. "We must be prepared to face it and ensure the forest's future."

Finn nodded, his eyes filled with resolve. "We have faced many challenges and grown stronger with each one," he said. "We are ready to face the final test and protect the forest."

Rowan's deep voice resonated with a sense of unity. "The forest has chosen us," he said. "We must trust in its wisdom and our own strength. Together, we can overcome any obstacle."

Thistle's eyes sparkled with excitement. "We have come a long way," she said. "But our journey is not over. We must continue to protect the forest and ensure the prophecy's fulfillment."

With renewed determination, Elara, Finn, Rowan, and Thistle set out to prepare for the final challenge. They knew that their bond as a group and their connection to the forest's magic would be crucial in overcoming the darkness that threatened the land.

As they trained, they felt a deep connection to the forest and its magic. The trees seemed to welcome them, their branches swaying gently in the breeze. The air was filled with the sounds of birds singing and leaves rustling, creating a symphony of nature's beauty.

Elara and Finn walked side by side, their bond stronger than ever. They had discovered hidden strengths within themselves, drawn from the forest's magic and their own determination.

"We have come a long way," Elara said, her voice filled with pride. "But our journey is not over. We must continue to protect the forest and uncover its secrets."

Finn nodded, his eyes filled with resolve. "We will face whatever challenges come our way," he said. "Together, we are unstoppable."

Rowan and Thistle walked behind them, their hearts filled with a sense of purpose and unity. They knew that they were part of something greater, protectors of a magical realm that held endless beauty and wisdom.

As they continued their journey, the whispers of the forest guided them, filling their minds with a sense of calm and clarity. They knew that the path ahead would be fraught with danger and deception, but they were ready to face whatever obstacles lay in their path.

One day, as they trained in a secluded glade, the whispers of the forest grew urgent, filling their minds with a sense of impending challenge. They knew that the time for the final test was approaching, and they needed to be ready.

"The prophecy speaks of a final challenge," Elara said, her voice filled with determination. "We must be prepared to face it and ensure the forest's future."

Finn nodded, his eyes filled with resolve. "We have faced many challenges and grown stronger with each one," he said. "We are ready to face the final test and protect the forest."

Rowan's deep voice resonated with a sense of unity. "The forest has chosen us," he said. "We must trust in its wisdom and our own strength. Together, we can overcome any obstacle."

Thistle's eyes sparkled with excitement. "We have come a long way," she said. "But our journey is not over. We must continue to protect the forest and ensure the prophecy's fulfillment."

With renewed determination, Elara, Finn, Rowan, and Thistle set out to prepare for the final challenge. They knew that their bond as a group and their connection to the forest's magic would be crucial in overcoming the darkness that threatened the land.

As they trained, they felt a deep connection to the forest and its magic. The trees seemed to welcome them, their branches swaying gently in the breeze. The air was filled with the sounds of birds singing and leaves rustling, creating a symphony of nature's beauty.

Elara and Finn walked side by side, their bond stronger than ever. They had discovered hidden strengths within themselves, drawn from the forest's magic and their own determination.

"We have come a long way," Elara said, her voice filled with pride. "But our journey is not over. We must continue to protect the forest and uncover its secrets."

Finn nodded, his eyes filled with resolve. "We will face whatever challenges come our way," he said. "Together, we are unstoppable."

Rowan and Thistle walked behind them, their hearts filled with a sense of purpose and unity. They knew that they were part of something greater, protectors of a magical realm that held endless beauty and wisdom.

As they continued their journey, the whispers of the forest guided them, filling their minds with a sense of calm and clarity. They knew that the path ahead would be fraught with danger and deception, but they were ready to face whatever obstacles lay in their path.

Their adventure was far from over, but they faced it with courage and determination. The Whispering Prophecy had given them new allies and powerful tools, and they were stronger for it. Together, they would protect the Whispering Forest and ensure that its magic and wisdom would endure for generations to come.

The glade with the ancient tree and the prophecy had revealed to them the true essence of their quest. It was not just about uncovering the prophecy but about discovering the strength within themselves and their bond with the forest. They had proven their worthiness, and now, with the prophecy in their possession, they had the guidance they needed to face the final challenge.

As they ventured deeper into the heart of the forest, the whispers grew clearer, guiding them toward their ultimate goal. They knew that their journey was far from over, but with the prophecy's guidance and the forest's wisdom, they felt ready to face whatever challenges lay ahead.

Elara, Finn, Rowan, and Thistle walked with renewed determination, their hearts filled with a sense of purpose and unity. The forest had chosen them as its protectors, and they were ready to fulfill that role with courage and dedication.

The path ahead was uncertain, but they knew that as long as they trusted in the forest's wisdom and their own strength, they could overcome any obstacle. Together, they would protect the Whispering Forest and ensure that its magic and beauty would endure for generations to come.

# Chapter 15: The Legacy of the Whispering Forest

The journey through the Whispering Forest had brought Elara, Finn, Rowan, and Thistle face to face with their deepest fears and greatest challenges. They had proven themselves time and again, gaining wisdom and strength from the ancient land. With the guidance of the Whispering Prophecy and the Silver Leaf, they were prepared to confront the ultimate challenge that would determine the fate of the forest. Their bravery, wisdom, and unity would be put to the test as they faced the darkness that threatened to consume the forest.

The morning air was filled with a sense of anticipation as they set out. The forest seemed to hold its breath, the trees whispering secrets and words of encouragement to the group. Vixen and Max stayed close, their keen senses on alert as they guided their human companions through the dense foliage.

Rowan spoke of the final challenge they were about to face, his deep voice resonating with a sense of urgency and determination.

"The prophecy foretells of a great darkness that will test us," Rowan began. "This darkness seeks to consume the forest's magic and plunge it into chaos. We must be prepared to face it with all our strength and unity."

Elara and Finn listened intently, their hearts filled with a mixture of fear and resolve. They knew that this final challenge would be their most difficult yet, but they were ready to face it together.

"The forest has guided us this far," Elara said, her voice steady. "We must trust in its wisdom and our own strength. We can overcome the darkness and restore balance to the forest."

Thistle's eyes sparkled with determination. "If we can defeat the darkness, the forest will be safe," she said. "We need to follow the prophecy and see this through to the end."

As they continued their journey, the whispers of the forest grew louder, urging them forward. The path led them to a secluded glade, bathed in the soft glow of the moonlight. In the center of the glade stood a tall, ancient tree with bark that seemed to shimmer with an ethereal light. The tree exuded an aura of wisdom and strength, and its presence filled the glade with a sense of calm and tranquility.

"This tree is special," Elara said, her voice filled with awe. "I can feel its power. It must be connected to the final challenge."

Rowan nodded, his eyes scanning the tree for any signs of a hidden message. "The tree may hold clues that can help us face the darkness," he said. "We need to look closely."

As they approached the tree, they noticed a series of intricate carvings etched into its bark. The carvings depicted scenes from the forest's history, from its creation to the present day. Each image was detailed and lifelike, telling the story of the forest's magic and the guardians who protected it.

Finn traced his fingers over the carvings, feeling a sense of connection to the forest. "These carvings are like a record of the forest's history," he said. "But there's something more here. Look at this."

He pointed to a section of the tree where the carvings seemed to form a pattern, creating a series of symbols and runes. The runes pulsed with a faint, blue light, as if holding a hidden message.

Elara examined the runes closely, her mind working to decipher their meaning. "The runes speak of a hidden path," she said. "A path that leads to the heart of the darkness. We need to follow these clues and find the hidden path."

Thistle's eyes sparkled with excitement. "This could be the key to facing the darkness," she said. "We should follow the runes and see where they lead."

Rowan nodded in agreement. "The forest is guiding us," he said. "We must trust in its wisdom and continue our journey."

With renewed determination, Elara, Finn, Rowan, and Thistle set out to follow the clues left by the runes. The whispers of the forest guided them, filling their minds with a sense of purpose and clarity. They knew that the journey ahead would be challenging, but they were ready to face whatever obstacles lay in their path.

As they ventured deeper into the forest, the runes led them to a series of hidden landmarks and ancient relics. Each clue brought them closer to confronting the darkness. They navigated treacherous terrain, crossed rushing rivers, and faced cunning creatures that sought to impede their progress. But with each trial, their bond grew stronger, and their determination never wavered.

One particularly difficult challenge came in the form of a dense, shadowy thicket that seemed to block their path. The thicket was filled with twisted vines and thorny bushes, creating a nearly impenetrable barrier. The whispers of the forest urged them to find a way through, but the path seemed impossible.

"We need to find a way around this thicket," Finn said, his voice filled with determination. "The heart of the darkness must be on the other side."

Rowan examined the thicket, his eyes scanning for any sign of a hidden path. "There must be a way through," he said. "We just need to find it."

Thistle darted ahead, her nimble form easily navigating the tangled vines. "I think I see something," she called out, pointing to a narrow gap in the thicket.

Elara and Finn followed Thistle, carefully making their way through the narrow gap. The vines scratched at their skin and clothing, but they pressed on, determined to reach the other side. Vixen and Max stayed close, their senses alert for any signs of danger.

After what felt like hours of struggling through the thicket, they finally emerged into a small clearing. The clearing was bathed in the soft glow of the moonlight, and in the center stood a tall, ancient tree with dark, shadowy leaves that seemed to absorb the light. The tree swayed gently, its branches forming a natural canopy that cast dappled shadows on the ground.

"This must be the place," Finn said, his voice filled with awe. "The place where we will face the darkness."

As they approached the tree, they felt a deep, resonant energy emanating from its trunk and branches. The whispers of the forest grew louder, filling their minds with a sense of calm and clarity. They knew that they were in the right place, and that the tree held the key to unlocking the final challenge.

"The runes on the tree must hold the key to unlocking the darkness," Rowan said, his voice filled with determination. "We need to decipher the runes and speak the words that will reveal the heart of the darkness."

Elara, Finn, Rowan, and Thistle examined the runes, their minds working to decipher their meaning. The runes were written in an ancient language, and they knew that they held the key to unlocking the tree's magic.

"The runes speak of balance and harmony, of light and dark," Elara said thoughtfully. "We need to find the right words to activate the tree's magic and reveal the heart of the darkness."

Rowan nodded, his eyes scanning the runes for any clues. "The tree is a guardian of the forest's wisdom," he said. "We need to speak the words of truth and purity to unlock its magic."

Thistle's eyes sparkled with excitement. "I recognize some of these runes," she said. "They speak of the ancient magic of the forest, of the balance between light and dark. We need to trust in the wisdom of the forest and speak the words that our hearts hold."

Elara and Finn joined hands, focusing their minds and hearts on the runes. They drew on the wisdom and strength of the forest, speaking the words that their hearts held.

"Ancient tree, guardian of the darkness's heart," Elara began, her voice steady and clear. "We seek the guidance and protection of the forest. We have come with pure intent and open hearts. Show us the way."

As Elara spoke the words, the runes began to glow with a soft, blue light. The ground beneath their feet seemed to hum with energy, and the tree's branches swayed gently, as if acknowledging their words.

"You have spoken the words of truth and purity," a deep, resonant voice said. "You have proven yourselves worthy of facing the darkness. The heart of the darkness will now be revealed to you."

The tree's dark, shadowy leaves began to shimmer and glow with an ethereal light. A hidden passage opened at the base of the tree, revealing a path that led deep underground.

"This passage leads to the heart of the darkness," the voice said. "It holds the essence of the forest's magic and the source of the darkness that threatens it. Use your wisdom and strength to overcome the final challenge and restore balance to the forest."

Elara and Finn stepped forward, their hearts filled with determination. They carefully entered the passage, feeling the warmth of the tree's magic guiding them.

"Thank you, guardian," Elara said, her voice filled with gratitude. "We will use our wisdom and strength to overcome the darkness and restore balance to the forest."

With renewed hope and strength, Elara, Finn, Rowan, and Thistle set out to face the final challenge. The whispers of the forest guided them, filling their minds with a sense of purpose and clarity. They knew that the journey ahead would be challenging, but they were ready to face whatever obstacles lay in their path.

As they ventured deeper into the underground passage, the air grew cooler and filled with an otherworldly energy. The walls of the passage were covered in intricate carvings and runes, telling the story of the forest's history and the guardians who protected it. The whispers of the forest grew louder, echoing through the passage and filling their minds with a sense of purpose and clarity.

After several minutes of walking, they emerged into a vast, cavernous chamber. The chamber was filled with a soft, blue light that seemed to emanate from the walls themselves. The air was thick with the presence of ancient magic, and the whispers of the forest echoed all around them.

"This is the heart of the darkness," Elara said, her voice filled with awe. "We need to use our wisdom and strength to overcome it and restore balance to the forest."

As they ventured deeper into the chamber, the whispers grew louder and more distinct. The voices of the ancient spirits seemed to call out to them, guiding them toward the source of the darkness.

In the center of the chamber stood a tall, imposing figure draped in dark, flowing robes. His hair was long and black, and his eyes glowed with an eerie, malevolent light. He exuded an aura of power and mystery, and his presence filled the chamber with a sense of tension and anticipation.

"Welcome, travelers," the figure said, his voice like the rustle of leaves in the wind. "I am Malachai, the Dark Sorcerer. I have been waiting for you."

Elara and Finn stepped forward, their hearts filled with a mixture of fear and determination. They knew that Malachai was the source of the darkness that threatened the forest, and they were ready to face him.

"We seek to restore balance to the forest," Elara said, her voice steady. "We will stand against you and protect the Whispering Forest."

Malachai's eyes narrowed, and a faint smile played at the corners of his lips. "Many have come seeking to challenge me," he said. "But few have proven themselves worthy. You must face my trials and earn my respect before I will grant you my aid."

Finn stepped forward, his eyes blazing with determination. "We are ready to face your trials," he said. "We will do whatever it takes to protect the forest."

Malachai's smile widened, and he raised his hands, casting a series of intricate spells. The air around them shimmered with magic, and the chamber was transformed into a labyrinth of twisting paths and hidden dangers.

"Your first trial is a test of courage and resolve," Malachai said. "You must navigate this labyrinth and reach the heart of the chamber. Only then will you prove yourselves worthy of my respect."

Elara, Finn, Rowan, and Thistle nodded, their hearts filled with determination. They knew that the labyrinth would be filled with challenges, but they were ready to face whatever obstacles lay ahead.

As they entered the labyrinth, the paths twisted and turned, creating a disorienting maze of rock and shadows. The air was thick with an otherworldly energy, and the whispers of the forest seemed to fade into the background.

"We need to stay together and trust in each other," Elara said, her voice steady. "The labyrinth is designed to test our courage and resolve. We must not lose our way."

Rowan nodded, his eyes scanning the paths for any sign of danger. "We need to keep moving and stay focused," he said. "The labyrinth is filled with traps and illusions. We must be vigilant."

Thistle darted ahead, her nimble form easily navigating the twisting paths. "I can sense the magic of the labyrinth," she said. "We need to follow the path of light. It will lead us to the heart of the chamber."

Elara and Finn followed Thistle, carefully making their way through the labyrinth. The paths were filled with hidden traps and illusions, designed to confuse and deceive them. They encountered shadowy figures that sought to block their way, but they stood their ground and pressed on, determined to reach the heart of the chamber.

As they ventured deeper into the labyrinth, they felt a growing sense of tension and anticipation. The paths grew darker and more twisted, and the air was filled with an eerie silence. They knew that they were nearing the heart of the chamber, and that the most difficult part of the trial lay ahead.

After what felt like hours of navigating the labyrinth, they reached a small clearing. In the center of the clearing stood a tall, ancient tree with dark, shadowy leaves that seemed to absorb the light. The tree swayed gently, its branches forming a natural canopy that cast dappled shadows on the ground.

"This must be the heart of the chamber," Finn said, his voice filled with awe. "We need to prove our worthiness to Malachai."

As they approached the tree, they felt a deep, resonant energy emanating from its trunk and branches. The whispers of the forest grew louder, filling their minds with a sense of calm and clarity. They knew that they were in the right place, and that the tree held the key to the next step of their journey.

Malachai appeared before them, his eyes glowing with an eerie, malevolent light. "You have reached the heart of the chamber," he said. "But your trials are not yet over. You must face one final test to prove your worthiness."

He raised his hands, casting a powerful spell that enveloped the clearing in a shimmering light. The ground beneath their feet seemed to hum with energy, and a series of ancient runes appeared on the trunk of the tree.

"This is a test of wisdom and insight," Malachai said. "You must decipher the runes and unlock the magic of the tree. Only then will you earn my respect and receive the artifact you seek."

Elara, Finn, Rowan, and Thistle examined the runes, their minds working to decipher their meaning. The runes were written in an ancient language, and they knew that they held the key to unlocking the tree's magic.

"The runes speak of balance and harmony, of light and dark," Elara said thoughtfully. "We need to find the right words to activate the tree's magic."

Rowan nodded, his eyes scanning the runes for any clues. "The tree is a guardian of the forest's wisdom," he said. "We need to speak the words of truth and purity to unlock its magic."

Thistle's eyes sparkled with excitement. "I recognize some of these runes," she said. "They speak of the ancient magic of the forest, of the balance between light and dark. We need to trust in the wisdom of the forest and speak the words that our hearts hold."

Elara and Finn joined hands, focusing their minds and hearts on the runes. They drew on the wisdom and strength of the forest, speaking the words that their hearts held.

"Ancient tree, guardian of the chamber's wisdom," Elara began, her voice steady and clear. "We seek the guidance and protection of the forest. We have come with pure intent and open hearts. Show us the way."

As Elara spoke the words, the runes began to glow with a soft, blue light. The ground beneath their feet seemed to hum with energy, and the tree's branches swayed gently, as if acknowledging their words.

"You have spoken the words of truth and purity," Malachai said, his voice filled with approval. "You have proven yourselves worthy of my respect. I will grant you the artifact you seek."

He raised his hands, casting a spell that caused the tree to shimmer and glow with an ethereal light. A small, intricately carved wooden box appeared at the base of the tree, its surface covered in ancient runes.

"This box contains a magical artifact that will aid you on your quest," Malachai said. "It holds the essence of the chamber's magic, a powerful tool that will help you protect the forest and stand against the darkness. Use it wisely and with respect."

Elara and Finn stepped forward, their hearts filled with gratitude and determination. They carefully picked up the wooden box, feeling its smooth surface and the warmth of its magic.

"Thank you, Malachai," Elara said, her voice filled with gratitude. "We will use the artifact to protect the forest and continue our quest."

Malachai smiled, his eyes twinkling with approval. "You have earned my respect and my guidance," he said. "The path to the heart of the forest lies before you. Follow the whispers and trust in the wisdom of the forest. You are ready to face whatever challenges lie ahead."

With renewed hope and strength, Elara, Finn, Rowan, and Thistle set out on the next leg of their journey, guided by the whispers and the wisdom of the forest. They knew that the path ahead would be fraught with danger and deception, but they were ready to face whatever obstacles lay in their path.

As they ventured deeper into the forest, they encountered a series of trials and challenges that tested their courage, intelligence, and bond with the land. They navigated treacherous terrain, crossed rushing rivers, and faced cunning creatures that sought to impede their progress. But with each trial, their bond grew stronger, and their determination never wavered.

Their adventure was far from over, but they faced it with courage and determination. The encounter with Malachai, the Dark Sorcerer, had given them new allies and powerful tools, and they were stronger for it. Together, they would protect the Whispering Forest and ensure that its magic and wisdom would endure for generations to come.

As they continued their journey, they felt a deep connection to the land and its magic. The trees seemed to welcome them, their branches swaying gently in the breeze. The air was filled with the sounds of birds singing and leaves rustling, creating a symphony of nature's beauty.

Elara and Finn walked side by side, their bond stronger than ever. They had discovered hidden strengths within themselves, drawn from the forest's magic and their own determination.

"We have come a long way," Elara said, her voice filled with pride. "But our journey is not over. We must continue to protect the forest and uncover its secrets."

Finn nodded, his eyes filled with resolve. "

We will face whatever challenges come our way," he said. "Together, we are unstoppable."

Rowan and Thistle walked behind them, their hearts filled with a sense of purpose and unity. They knew that they were part of something greater, protectors of a magical realm that held endless beauty and wisdom.

As they continued their journey, the whispers of the forest guided them, filling their minds with a sense of calm and clarity. They knew that the path ahead would be fraught with danger and deception, but they were ready to face whatever obstacles lay in their path.

One day, as they trained in a secluded glade, the whispers of the forest grew urgent, filling their minds with a sense of impending challenge. They knew that the time for the final test was approaching, and they needed to be ready.

"The prophecy speaks of a final challenge," Elara said, her voice filled with determination. "We must be prepared to face it and ensure the forest's future."

Finn nodded, his eyes filled with resolve. "We have faced many challenges and grown stronger with each one," he said. "We are ready to face the final test and protect the forest."

Rowan's deep voice resonated with a sense of unity. "The forest has chosen us," he said. "We must trust in its wisdom and our own strength. Together, we can overcome any obstacle."

Thistle's eyes sparkled with excitement. "We have come a long way," she said. "But our journey is not over. We must continue to protect the forest and ensure the prophecy's fulfillment."

With renewed determination, Elara, Finn, Rowan, and Thistle set out to prepare for the final challenge. They knew that their bond as a group and their connection to the forest's magic would be crucial in overcoming the darkness that threatened the land.

As they trained, they felt a deep connection to the forest and its magic. The trees seemed to welcome them, their branches swaying gently in the breeze. The air was filled with the sounds of birds singing and leaves rustling, creating a symphony of nature's beauty.

Elara and Finn walked side by side, their bond stronger than ever. They had discovered hidden strengths within themselves, drawn from the forest's magic and their own determination.

"We have come a long way," Elara said, her voice filled with pride. "But our journey is not over. We must continue to protect the forest and uncover its secrets."

Finn nodded, his eyes filled with resolve. "We will face whatever challenges come our way," he said. "Together, we are unstoppable."

Rowan and Thistle walked behind them, their hearts filled with a sense of purpose and unity. They knew that they were part of something greater, protectors of a magical realm that held endless beauty and wisdom.

As they continued their journey, the whispers of the forest guided them, filling their minds with a sense of calm and clarity. They knew that the path ahead would be fraught with danger and deception, but they were ready to face whatever obstacles lay in their path.

Their adventure was far from over, but they faced it with courage and determination. The encounter with Malachai had given them new allies and powerful tools, and they were stronger for it. Together, they would protect the Whispering Forest and ensure that its magic and wisdom would endure for generations to come.

The glade with the ancient tree and the prophecy had revealed to them the true essence of their quest. It was not just about uncovering the prophecy but about discovering the strength within themselves and their bond with the forest. They had proven their worthiness, and now, with the prophecy in their possession, they had the guidance they needed to face the final challenge.

As they ventured deeper into the heart of the forest, the whispers grew clearer, guiding them toward their ultimate goal. They knew that their journey was far from over, but with the prophecy's guidance and the forest's wisdom, they felt ready to face whatever challenges lay ahead.

Elara, Finn, Rowan, and Thistle walked with renewed determination, their hearts filled with a sense of purpose and unity. The forest had chosen them as its protectors, and they were ready to fulfill that role with courage and dedication.

The path ahead was uncertain, but they knew that as long as they trusted in the forest's wisdom and their own strength, they could overcome any obstacle. Together, they would protect the Whispering Forest and ensure that its magic and beauty would endure for generations to come.

Their adventure was far from over, but they faced it with courage and determination. The encounter with Malachai had given them new allies and powerful tools, and they were stronger for it. Together, they would protect the Whispering Forest and ensure that its magic and wisdom would endure for generations to come.

The glade with the ancient tree and the prophecy had revealed to them the true essence of their quest. It was not just about uncovering the prophecy but about discovering the strength within themselves and their bond with the forest. They had proven their worthiness, and now, with the prophecy in their possession, they had the guidance they needed to face the final challenge.

As they ventured deeper into the heart of the forest, the whispers grew clearer, guiding them toward their ultimate goal. They knew that their journey was far from over, but with the prophecy's guidance and the forest's wisdom, they felt ready to face whatever challenges lay ahead.

Elara, Finn, Rowan, and Thistle walked with renewed determination, their hearts filled with a sense of purpose and unity. The forest had chosen them as its protectors, and they were ready to fulfill that role with courage and dedication.

The path ahead was uncertain, but they knew that as long as they trusted in the forest's wisdom and their own strength, they could overcome any obstacle.

Together, they would protect the Whispering Forest and ensure that its magic and beauty would endure for generations to come.

Their adventure was far from over, but they faced it with courage and determination. The final challenge lay ahead, and they were ready to face it with all the wisdom and strength they had gained. Together, they would protect the Whispering Forest and ensure that its legacy endured for generations to come.

# Don't miss out!

Visit the website below and you can sign up to receive emails whenever Patrick William Lee publishes a new book. There's no charge and no obligation.

https://books2read.com/r/B-A-FLRYB-ZARZD

**BOOKS2READ**

Connecting independent readers to independent writers.

# About the Author

Patrick William Lee is a renowned author celebrated for his enchanting tales of magic and wonder. Specializing in the genres of fairy tales, folk tales, legends, and mythology, Patrick weaves stories that transport readers to fantastical realms where the impossible becomes reality. With a deep love for folklore and a talent for crafting timeless narratives, his books captivate the imaginations of readers young and old. When he's not writing, Patrick enjoys exploring ancient forests, studying mythical creatures, and sharing his passion for storytelling with audiences around the world. His works continue to inspire and delight, leaving a lasting impact on the world of literature.